DIRTY PROMISES

AUBREY BONDURANT

Cover by Elizabeth Kelly
ISBN: 979-8750124855

This book is for mature audiences only.

Chapter One

OAKLEY

Clothes being shed. My body on display, perspiration peppering my skin.

My hands are tied. A blindfold over my eyes heightened all of my other senses. A man is worshipping every inch of my body.

People are watching.

Although I can't see them, I can feel them staring at the scene as it unfolds. Their desire in watching me fuels my ultimate fantasy.

I woke with a start, tangled in my bedsheets and completely alone. The sound of rain on my bedroom window pulled me slowly from the lingering shadows of my dream back to reality.

Fuck. My recurring dream had grown more vivid in recent nights, mocking me for something I could never have. Familiar shame washed over me. I was a good girl who'd had three sexual partners, not a deviant who got off on people watching her have sex.

Besides, hadn't I already learned the hard way what happens when you try to push the limits of what's considered normal in a relationship? Although it had been eight months, the judgment from my ex-boyfriend and the lasting fallout still stung.

After rolling out of bed, I got up to take a quick shower, anxious to get the day moving. I had a big weekend ahead. Getting packed was the first order of business. When the phone rang, I answered with a smile.

"Hello," I greeted Kate, my childhood best friend. I switched the call over to my ear pods so I could pack my suitcase while talking to her. My bridesmaid dress and shoes were pulled out of my closet first since they were the most essential items for the weekend.

"Hi, you all packed?"

"Working on it as we speak."

"You're not packed already? I hope you don't forget anything for the wedding."

I had to bite my tongue at her tone, which had turned judgey lately. There was plenty of time for me to pack this morning before my ride picked me up. On top of that, I'd worked a forty-hour week in three days in order to take the upcoming two days off for her wedding.

The difference in our goals had created tension over the last few months. Maybe this was typical when best friends started to grow apart. When one stayed in their hometown and the other moved away.

"Don't worry. I won't forget anything."

"I'm excited to see you."

"Me too." And I genuinely was. Kate had lived across the street when I was growing up, and her house had provided a safe haven during my teenage years when my parents seemed to be more concerned about fighting than about their only child. Then when my mom and dad had divorced during my senior year, Kate's family had allowed me to stay with them to finish out high school, so I wasn't forced to move during such an important time of my life. I owed a great deal to Kate and her family.

"How are things with Shawn?" she asked, changing the subject.

"Going well." Shawn was a college friend of Kate's fiancé. A month ago, she'd set us up when he'd moved to the city. We'd been out on three dates over the last three weeks, and I liked him, but I was also cautious. After my last relationship had ended in a humiliation of epic proportion, I wasn't exactly eager for another. And there was also something about Shawn I couldn't quite put my finger on.

"I know you're thinking about what happened with Evan."

The name made me cringe even eight months later. I'd thought I could trust him, but in the end, he'd betrayed me.

"But you need to get back out there, and what better way than by sharing a hotel room with Shawn this weekend?"

"Yeah, it's a big step." The rooms were expensive at the wedding venue, but even so I hadn't been ready to share one with Shawn. Then he'd suggested a suite with two beds so as not to pressure me and I'd cautiously agreed.

"Hopefully in a couple years, it'll be you two getting married."

Dude, it had been three dates. She needed to slow her roll. Ever since Kate had gotten engaged, she'd been ready for all her friends to take the plunge. And since she and her fiancé were responsible for setting me up with Shawn, she seemed even more anxious for us to work out.

In her mind, she wanted all of her friends to get married, move to upstate New York, and have babies together in the small town we'd grown up in. I shuddered at the thought. I was two years out of college and just starting in my career.

Small-town living with the people she'd grown up with might be her idea of happiness, but it certainly wasn't mine.

After moving to the Big Apple, I'd become electrified by the energy of the city. I loved my job as a marketing coordinator. Sure, my salary might be small, my apartment even smaller, but I was happy with my life here.

Since my parents had moved to different states after their divorce, there was less reason for me to return to our home town these days. Especially in January. Speaking of which: "How much snow is on the ground?"

"At least a couple inches with more forecasted. I want fresh snow for my fairy-tale wedding day."

She was getting married at a beautiful venue, so a snowy backdrop would be perfect. "I'll be sure to pack my boots."

"Make sure you pack sexy lingerie too."

Did a lacy black bra and matching thong count? I didn't own any real lingerie. Nor did I have the funds to spring for anything fancy. In my limited experience, men seemed to prefer naked to anything else. Here was hoping if I did in fact decide to sleep with Shawn, he wouldn't be picky about my attire.

"Oh my God, I almost forgot to tell you. Max is coming to the wedding."

My pulse leapt at the name of her older brother. Max was the type of guy crushes were invented for. All of Kate's friends had drooled over him while we were growing up. He'd been a senior in high school when we'd been in the awkward middle school years and only just discovering boys. He'd always been nice to me, considering Kate and I were often joined at the hip, but he'd never paid me much attention otherwise.

"Great news. Will there be tension?"

Max and their parents had gone through a big falling

out years ago. No one talked about it. The only thing I'd ever gleaned from Kate was that her parents didn't agree with his life choices, whatever that meant. But it was good to know he'd be there on such an important day for his baby sister.

"There may be some stress. To be honest, I'm surprised Max accepted the invitation. Hopefully, I don't come to regret it."

No one wanted a bride to be upset during her wedding. I hoped everyone would put aside their differences for the weekend. "I'm sure it'll be fine."

"Yeah. Hope so. I've gotta go. My mom is stressing out about the table arrangements. I can't wait to see you tonight."

"I can't wait, either. See you then."

After disconnecting the call, I finished packing everything I would need and grabbed a cereal bar, figuring we'd grab lunch somewhere along the way. I was ready to go by the time Shawn texted to let me know he was outside.

Great timing. I threw my heavy coat over my arm, knowing I'd need it at some point, and turned off the lights to my studio apartment. All ready.

Shawn's shiny red BMW was parked outside at the curb. I assumed he'd get out and help me with my suitcase and garment bag. Instead, I heard the sound of his trunk popping open.

Okay. Not exactly gentlemanly, but once I slid into the passenger seat, I could see he was on a call.

I expected an apologetic smile, but instead he held a finger to his lips as if I needed a reminder to keep quiet. I could easily hear the conversation being broadcast over the speaker. Though I disliked being treated like an intruder, I dismissed Shawn's behavior as the result of stress from his job as a financial advisor. However, I didn't appreciate his glare as I quietly pulled my seat belt over. The click as it caught was not in my control.

Sitting in the passenger seat, careful not to move a muscle or breathe too loudly while he conducted a work call was not my idea of the start to a romantic weekend. I forced myself to relax, however, and took the opportunity to let my mind wander. Car rides were the absolute best for allowing me to decompress, and since this one was at least four hours, there would be plenty of time to do so. I liked my job in marketing at the Manhattan firm, but between the ten-hour days and commuting from Jersey to Manhattan, it left little time to unwind.

I turned to study Shawn. He was handsome in a clean-cut, former-frat-boy, probably-spent-too-much-time-on-his-hair kind of way. He'd been charming over our last three dates. Held open doors, paid for dinners, and kissed me good night without any pressure for more.

Yet I couldn't help but wonder if it was an act. The guy seemed to have a veneer to him. A fakeness of sorts. I knew this was a jaded way of viewing someone who'd done nothing wrong, but I couldn't help myself.

After thirty minutes, Shawn finally ended his work call.

"Sorry about the call. The guys at work can't do a thing without me." He put his hand on my knee and squeezed.

His tone rubbed me the wrong way. From the conversation I'd overheard, he'd forgotten to do something before taking off for the long weekend. I took a deep breath. Whatever. It wasn't my concern. We had an entire weekend to look forward to.

Tonight, we had informal plans to meet the bride and groom-to-be for drinks. The rehearsal and dinner would be tomorrow, and the wedding on Saturday. Then we'd drive home Sunday morning after brunch. Plenty of time for us to get to know each other better. "Hopefully you won't have to work once we get there."

"No way. I can't wait to spend all my time with you."

When he touched my thigh, there were no butterflies, zings, or chills. This wasn't boding well. Not even his suave good-night kisses could make my heart race or my chest burn with pent-up desire.

Then again, had anyone achieved that feat? Not if I was being honest. How sad to think the best erotic experience of my life had been in a dream.

At least Shawn had been patient and never pressured me into moving too fast. I wanted to take this weekend to get to know him. Three dates on Saturday nights where you put your best foot forward in a crowded restaurant wasn't a test of compatibility. But this weekend definitely would be.

I tried to recall what had attracted me to Shawn in the first place. His boyish smile. The fact he already knew my friends and was part of the group. The way his teeth were perfectly straight and white.

My eyes rolled internally. Jesus. That was ad copy for a toothpaste commercial, not the makings of a lasting attraction.

When small talk turned to the wedding of our best friends, I relaxed. My ease only lasted one more hour when we hit traffic on the highway.

"Fuck. This is going to take forever." He banged the steering wheel with frustration.

I hadn't expected traffic leaving mid-morning on a Thursday, either, but we weren't in a hurry, and it was probably just an accident. "It's all right. GPS says it clears in a mile."

But Shawn wasn't appeased. My eyes went wide when he pulled off to the right shoulder and began to drive there.

"Good, we'll go around. If we get pulled over, pretend you're having an emergency."

"Wh-at?" I couldn't believe it. He was illegally driving on the shoulder of the road. Although I was all for bending some laws, like edging over the speed limit and the occasional jaywalk on an empty street, this was extreme. "Shawn, we're not in a hurry. I don't want you to get pulled over."

He glared at me. "I need to get to the room so I can log in to the Wi-Fi and finish up something for the office."

So much for not having to do more work. I hissed through my teeth when he slammed on his brakes. My foot was on an imaginary one, my entire body tense.

He started cursing, and I realized we'd stopped because of an accident on the shoulder which was now blocking his way. He swerved back into the lane of traffic, causing the car he'd almost clipped to honk.

"Motherfuckers," he shouted, now cutting off a large SUV to move another lane to the left. "Finally," he yelled in triumph when we reached the left travel lane, only to hit gridlock again.

I sensed what was about to happen next. "Please don't drive on the shoulder again. This will clear up."

He snapped, "I don't need a backseat driver."

I retorted, "And I don't need some road-raging maniac asking me to make up emergencies for driving illegally."

He swiftly swung onto the left shoulder, but instead of speeding ahead, he slammed on the brakes. "Get out, then."

"What?" My eyes went wide. He couldn't be serious.

His face was red, his expression angry. "You don't like my driving. Get the fuck out of my car."

Who was this guy? Yet my gut told me this was what I hadn't been able to put my finger on. This was what his veneer had been covering. A road-raging jerk with anger issues.

I yanked my coat from the backseat and grabbed my purse from the floor by my feet. No way was I putting up with this asshole a moment longer. I'd call an Uber. "Fine."

After climbing out the passenger door, I walked toward the trunk to retrieve my things, but he had other ideas. Peeling out, he threw up gravel and other road debris in his wake. I yelped with pain when sharp rock fragments peppered my face, coughed at the dust, and stared at the rear of his BMW in complete shock.

Chapter Two

MAX

"When are you leaving?"

I looked up from my desk toward my best friend and business partner, Shane. "Half hour ago."

He shook his head. "You promised your sister you'd be there."

My hand scrubbed over my face. "Believe me. I know. But maybe it would be better if I just went for the wedding ceremony instead of the full weekend. I have some work I could get done."

"No, you don't. The club will be fine without you. Something you told me how many times while I was on my honeymoon?"

As if on cue, Daniella, his wife of six months, stepped off the elevator. She had eyes only for her husband, who returned her intent gaze in full. When she walked up, and he took her face between his hands, I felt like a third wheel.

They made a stunning couple. She, with long, flame-colored hair twisted up in a bun and a brilliant smile. He, dark-haired, brooding, yet softening at the sight of his love.

A pang of jealousy hit me. It wasn't that I didn't enjoy

seeing my best friend and his beautiful wife happy, but I wished I had someone look at me the way Dani looked at Shane.

She was unconcerned he was half-owner of a sex club. Undeterred by his gruff exterior and hard edges. And the best thing to ever happen to him.

Her gaze fell on me, her expression confused. “I thought you’d be on the road by now, Max.”

“I had to get the liquor order in before I left.”

She chuckled at my lame excuse. “Come on. It won’t be too bad going home, will it?”

“I haven’t spoken to my parents in eleven years.”

Although I’d always known my father had the idea I’d follow in his footsteps in the family law business, I hadn’t expected him and my mom to cut me off completely for making a different choice. After my dad found out about my ownership in a sex club, he’d called me a disgrace. Yes, a sex club would be tough for any parent to accept, but he’d made it sound as if I was a horrible human for choosing this lifestyle. As if I’d gone against a moral code I didn’t remember him having until it suited him. I think what hurt the most was having my mother go along with it.

It didn’t matter all the years I’d been a loving son, brother, and member of the family. As of eleven years ago, I was no longer considered part of the unit.

But when my little sister, Kate, had called and invited me to her wedding, it had meant a lot. I wouldn’t miss her special day for anything, which meant I’d swallowed the hurt and resentment and said yes.

Daniella came over and set a hand on my shoulder. “I’m sorry, Max. But fuck them. You’ll go for your sister, ignore anyone who’s an asshole, and return here on Sunday to your real family.”

Shane and Dani were like family. Hell, all the people who worked here at the club were a type of surrogate family. It was a place people came for acceptance and freedom. I was proud for creating such a judgment-free zone, even if years later I privately struggled with my own demons when it came to self-acceptance. Visiting home would only heighten my doubts. "Thank you. Call me if you need me to come back early."

Shane shook his head. "Nice try. Everything is good. We have the new manager who's doing great."

Yes, Dylan was a godsend. He made it possible for us owners to take more time off. "You're right he is doing great. He's taking my Valentine's Day performance slot this year, by the way."

Shane nodded, not seeming surprised by the substitution. To the outside world, owning and partaking in a sex club would be a dream come true. Hell, in my twenties, I'd taken full advantage, performing whenever and with whomever was up for it. But over the last year, I'd started to feel burned out. Perhaps I was getting older and the novelty was wearing off. Or maybe it was watching Shane and Daniella's relationship grow and feeling unfulfilled with meaningless sex. Who knew. But whatever it was causing my funk, it helped to have supportive friends.

"Okay." I stood up. "Time to go."

Ninety minutes later, I hit gridlock. From the looks of it, there was an accident off to the right. I winced at the sight of the crunched cars and hoped everyone was okay. At least the police were already on the scene. I was about to move forward when a red Beemer came racing up from the shoulder and cut in front of me, causing me to hit the brakes and spill my coffee. I laid on the horn to voice my displeasure. "Prick."

Watching him cut the next car off and weave ahead, I shook my head and hoped karma would catch up with the asshole. I inched forward past the accident, able to speed up for only a short time before I was forced to slow down again. I didn't mind. At least now when I told my sister traffic made me late, it wouldn't be a lie.

My gaze roamed ahead, discovering the red BMW pulled over on the left shoulder. How poetic would a flat tire be? Would serve him right, especially in this cold weather. I watched as the passenger door opened, and a woman got out. Shutting the door, she walked toward the rear of the vehicle. Without warning, the car peeled out, sending a cloud of dust and rock flying towards the poor girl who shielded herself with her hands.

Are you fucking kidding me? I didn't hesitate to move over to the shoulder and pull up behind her.

Chapter Three

OAKLEY

I stood there stunned, my breath visible in the crisp air. What in the hell had just happened? Three dates might not have been enough time for me to have determined the meaning behind his red flags, but how could Kate's fiancé be good friends with a psycho?

Quickly, I shrugged into my coat, already shivering with the cold. Meanwhile, a gray SUV pulled onto the shoulder. Although I was grateful someone would stop for me, I wasn't about to get into a vehicle with a random stranger. I pulled out my phone, searching for my Uber app. I heard the door of the SUV open and the crunch of gravel under the stranger's shoes.

"Miss. Are you okay?" the masculine voice asked.

I turned around, about to tell him I was fine when words failed me. Damn. Serial killers couldn't be that good looking, right? He was tall, with sandy-brown hair and a handsome face. One which looked familiar?

"Max?"

His eyes went wide, and he stopped in his tracks. "Yes. Have we met?"

I exhaled a sigh of relief. “Yeah, I’d say so. I’m Oakley, Kate’s friend. We were seven years apart in school.”

He grinned, his dimples amping up his good looks by a factor of a thousand percent. Max might be in his thirties now, but he still had the same boyish, crush-worthy charm about him as when he’d been a teenager.

“Little Oakley Winters. You’re all grown up.”

“I am.” My arms hugged my waist in an attempt to keep myself warm.

“And stuck on the side of the road by an asshole.”

“Yep.” Much to my humiliation.

“Come on. You can tell me all about it from my warm car.”

An offer way too good to pass up. “Thanks.”

I’d never been more grateful for heat than once I got into Max’s SUV. He made sure I was buckled in before pulling into traffic. “Assuming you’re going my way?”

“I am indeed. You staying at the Burgess Hotel?”

“Yes. Kate made me a reservation.” He didn’t exactly look thrilled about it.

Watching Max drive was a treat. It gave me the chance to take in the man he’d become over the last decade. Broad shoulders, fine lines by his eyes, and a slight stubble on his face. Teenage Max had nothing on the Thirty-Something-Year-Old version.

“The asshole in the Beemer your boyfriend?”

“No. Shawn and I dated briefly, but no longer. Unfortunately, he’s in the wedding too.”

“What the hell happened? Aside from him driving like a crazy person?”

“He turned into a road-raging jerk when we hit gridlock. When I said something about not wanting to fake an emergency if we got pulled over, he got even angrier. Then I asked for him not to drive on the shoulder again, and he told me if I didn't like it, to get the fuck out. He still has my clothes."

"I'm going to kill him."

Holy level-ten hotness. Max would have to go and say something all alpha. He'd pushed all my turn-on buttons in one gruff statement. "Take a number. He sprayed me with gravel." I brought down the visor and opened up the mirror to inspect the damage. A couple nicks on my right cheek stood out.

"Let me see."

We were stopped again in traffic, so Max could safely take his gaze off the road to inspect my face. This. This was butterflies, zings, and a lot of blood rushing to all the inappropriate places. The intensity was off the charts, and then he had to go and push me into a territory I shall call, "*please don't groan, swoon, or pant*" when he gently touched my face.

"Killing the bastard is too quick for what he deserves."

My entire body shivered. I don't know if I was relieved or disappointed when traffic started to move, and he had to remove his fingers and divert his gaze.

I let out the breath I was holding. It was for the best his attention was back on the road.

One did not stare at the sun without going blind.

MAX

My rage over the way Shawn the douche had treated Oakley was only tempered by my unexpected attraction to her.

She was adorable. Yep, adorable was a word I was sticking to in order to remind myself she was my little sister's best friend. The girl who'd sat many a night at our dining room table with her frizzy dark hair and shy smile. She'd spent so many nights at our house people often assumed I had two younger sisters.

But damn if she hadn't blossomed into a beautiful woman with her long ebony locks, full lips, and incredible, honey-brown eyes.

Nope. I wouldn't go there. She was all of what? Twenty-four, and guaranteed much too innocent for the likes of me. She, like my sister, was probably looking for a husband by twenty-five, and kids by thirty. I shuddered at the suburban dream most women from my small town desired. More like a nightmare if you asked me.

"When is the last time you've been home?" she inquired.

"Eleven years ago." Over a decade since I'd been called a

disgrace to the family. Since I'd become the son who'd not only let my father down by dropping out of law school, but who'd also gone and thrown his life away by owning and working at a sex club. It was unforgivable in his eyes. And the punishment had been banishment for life.

You would think after all these years it would sting less. I suppose it did on a daily basis, where I had no reminders of my father's rejection in the life I'd built in New York City. But on the road home, all of the past resentments and insecurities bubbled up.

As if sensing my trepidation, she sighed. "I'm sorry. Kate never said what caused the fallout with your folks, but I'm sure whatever it was doesn't make it easy to come home after all these years."

Say what now? Until this moment, I'd assumed my reputation had been dragged through the mud all over my small town. It hadn't occurred to me that my parents would never utter a word about it. I should've been relieved. But instead I was—what? Disappointed? They apparently didn't talk about me at all.

"My sister never mentioned anything?"

I didn't miss the pretty blush on her cheeks indicating there might be more to the story. "Something about a disagreement over your life choices. She might know the details, but she never told me. I kind of assumed it had something to do with you deciding not to become a lawyer like your dad?"

"Yeah, dropping out of law school was certainly part of it." When Kate had first asked what had happened, she'd been so young and naïve. I hadn't dared tell her about the club. Then over the years, she'd stopped asking, and I assumed she'd found out the truth on her own. We stayed in touch on birthdays and holidays, but other than her occasional trip to the city, we didn't see each other much.

I was grateful Oakley didn't know about the club even if the idea of such an innocent experiencing it for the first time made my dick hard. Nope, not going there. Not only would she be shocked to her core, but if there was one woman off-limits this weekend, it was the one my parents considered like a second daughter.

Time for a subject change. "Where are you living these days?"

"In Jersey City, but I commute into Manhattan each day."

I was surprised to hear she was living near the city but admonished myself against any thoughts about seeing her again in the future. "What led you to the Big Apple?"

"I went to college at NYU and enjoyed the city enough to stay. Of course it's ridiculously expensive, so I'm in Jersey City and commute. But I feel good about my marketing firm and my career trajectory there."

Huh, she surprised me again with the focus on career. "Your parents still live in town?"

"No. They split during my senior year. I actually stayed with your parents so I could finish my final year of high school."

"Kate mentioned it, I think." After living together, she and my sister had to be pretty close.

"Both my parents are remarried. My dad lives in Florida with his wife and her two younger kids, and my mom is in California with her new husband, although they travel to Mexico quite a bit."

"Must be strange to no longer have your family live where you grew up."

"It was at first, but even though our small town was a great place to grow up, it doesn't do it for me anymore. I don't mean any offense, and please don't tell Kate, but I'm happier to travel to LA or Miami than to drive up here."

More surprises. I'd also been anxious to leave small-town living behind. New York City had represented excitement to a college kid, but now it represented home. I loved the energy and bustle, not to mention the diversity of people who lived there. It allowed everyone to find their place instead of forcing you into a predesigned notion of where you should fit in.

After an hour of easy conversation between us, my stomach growled. It was past lunchtime, and I'd skipped breakfast. "You hungry?"

"Definitely. What do you have in mind?"

"Let's pull off this exit and see what they have."

I knew many a woman who would've complained about sandwiches from a gas station deli, but not Oakley. She was inhaling a chicken parmesan sandwich without apology. I grinned, taking a large bite of my steak and cheese.

"Good?" she asked.

"Not bad, but not as good as a street vendor by my condo. Guy is from Philly and doesn't mess around with his cheesesteak sandwiches." The place stayed open until the wee hours, so I could hit it right after closing the club to obtain the very best comfort food.

"Cheez Whiz or provolone?"

I smiled. "Cheez Whiz of course. And the onion rings are incredible. They're smothered in cheese too."

"You'll have to give me his location. I'm always in search of great street food."

I had the sudden urge to invite her over, and we could order in one night. Dangerous thoughts. I'd already reasoned she was off-limits. It wasn't as if I was boyfriend material anyhow with my long hours spent at the club.

It took another three hours to get to the hotel. After parking, I found myself reluctant to get out of my SUV. As if Oakley sensed it, she reached over and squeezed my hand. "I hope you know how much it means to Kate to have you here. So no matter what else happens, please remember that. Also, I'm forever in your debt for the roadside rescue."

Her gesture was one of comfort, yet I could feel my pulse race at the contact. What the hell was happening to me? I wasn't a man who got excited from a simple touch. Hell, until this moment, I'd have argued I'd become desensitized to all forms of contact outside of the sexual act itself.

I cleared my throat, an unnamed emotion threatening to take hold. "You're right. This weekend is all about Kate. Let's get checked in and find the asshole in the red Beemer to get your things."

I had some choice things to say to Shawn, but afterward, I was eager to go hide in my hotel room and minimize my exposure to the family.

The hotel lobby was made up of shiny, wood-paneled walls, marble floors, and a large reception area filled with plush carpets and leather couches. Swank chandeliers gave it extra class. It wasn't so different from my club, although people were wearing a lot more clothing.

One of the walls leading to the check-in desk was lined with a wine rack from floor to ceiling, one edge of a glass-enclosed tasting room.

I noticed Oakley zero in on a preppy blond guy at the reception desk. He was getting a hotel room key from the clerk and had two small suitcases at his feet, one of them pink along with two garment bags draped over them.

He turned, and as if he'd forgotten about the circumstances which had Oakley walking in with me instead of him, he smiled. "Just in time. Here's your key."

She snatched her suitcase and bag. "I don't think so. I'm not sharing a room with you."

He rolled his eyes. "Come on. I was going to turn around to get you."

"When? Over three hours ago when you left me on the side of the freeway in freezing cold temperatures and sprayed me with gravel? I don't think so." She turned to the front desk clerk. "I'd like a room, please. One as far away from this asshole as possible."

The clerk shook her head. "I'm so sorry, miss, but we're booked up for the weekend. I've heard the Hampton Inn in town has some openings."

Town was eight miles away. Oakley's face falling while Shawn chuckled was unacceptable. Before I could question what I was doing, I pushed forward.

Chapter Five

OAKLEY

My bravado in telling Shawn off was completely wiped out by the front desk clerk's news about the lack of rooms. I should've called from the road to ask for my own room instead of assuming they'd have one available once I arrived. Shawn's glee over my predicament was enough to send me into a fit of rage or tears. I wasn't sure which would win out when Max stepped forward.

Nothing like having him witness my humiliation twice in the same day.

But his words were shocking. "Oakley can stay with me." He turned toward the front desk clerk. "The reservation is under Max Brooks."

Shawn's face turned red. "What? Who the hell are you?" He focused on Max for the first time.

"I'm the man who's about to have a little talk with you about what's an acceptable way to treat women."

Shawn's face flushed, and—no surprise—he looked nervous as hell. Max was a large man compared to him. And the way Max's voice did this edge-of-danger thing… Yeah, it was ridiculously hot—I mean intimidating for Shawn. *Jesus, Oakley, get it together.*

"This was just a misunderstanding. It isn't your business," Shawn sputtered.

Max remained calm, but the tone of menace stayed in his voice. "Oh, but it is."

The front desk clerk bounced her gaze around the three of us. "Um, Mr. Brooks, do you have a credit card?"

"Yes, I do. And I'd like two keys, please."

Shawn's eyes went wide, and I realized he was staring at the black American Express card. Huh, guess Max had money. Not something I cared about, but definitely high on Shawn's list, judging by the envy in his expression. Another red flag. Maybe I should've seen it before when he'd always made a point of ordering the most expensive thing on the menu.

Max handed me a room key, signed a sheet of paper, and we finished up quickly. He put his credit card back in his money clip and stepped toward Shawn. "Apologize to the lady for dumping her on the side of the road."

Shawn sneered, his gaze focusing on me. Evidently the mask was off and so were the gloves. "The only reason I dated you was as a favor to Kate. Which was a big favor considering high school girls put out faster than you do."

"That's enough." Max spoke with authority. He leaned down close to Shawn's ear to whisper something. I couldn't hear his words, but by the way they registered in Shawn's expression, I could imagine the creativity.

Max stepped back with a smile which didn't meet his eyes. "Let's go, Oakley."

He didn't give me the chance to respond, taking my arm and leading me to the elevator. I was thankful he'd taken charge as my body hadn't yet caught up to my brain.

Once we were alone in the elevator with the doors still open, he grinned. "You know what this moment calls for, don't you?"

My gaze bounced from him to an angry Shawn staring at us. "What's that?"

He pulled me close in a lover's embrace. "Less stunned, more excited to touch me, darlin'. Unless you don't want to."

My eyes went wide. Was this real life or had I slipped into a romance-novel fantasy?

His warm body was real. His intense blue eyes were real. The humming of my body was real. Max was rescuing me by allowing me to give Shawn a big *fuck you* in the best way possible. It was now or never.

I chose now. His lips barely brushed mine at first. But the chaste kiss wouldn't do. As if we both were spurred on by the first taste, we moved at once to deepen the kiss. Damn. No worries about missing butterflies, chills, or a spark with this man. All three hit me at once.

An involuntary moan left my throat when his tongue touched mine. I vaguely recognized the floor moving beneath my feet, but it wasn't until the distinctive elevator ding sounded and the doors opened that I realized we'd arrived on our floor.

Max was first to break the contact, stepping away with a twinkle in his eye. "Guess we showed him."

"Who?" Oh, damn, Shawn. Right. The entire reason for the "fake" kiss.

He chuckled. "Come on. Let's find our room."

Our. He said it so casually, as if he hadn't just rocked my world.

Max took my hand, the contact seemingly natural. With one swipe of his hotel room key, the door opened and we entered.

My eyes immediately fell upon the giant four-poster, king-sized bed. Jesus, the one-room, one-bed thing keeping in line with the feel of a romance novel. Now if only the power would go out, so we were forced to snuggle for warmth. Yep, I was one step away from developing a whole new fantasy.

"I should've asked for two beds. It slipped my mind." He stood there gripping his neck.

Chapter Six

MAX

The grand idea of wiping the smug look off of Shawn's face had suddenly been doused with the reality of sharing a hotel room with a beautiful woman who was off-limits.

Not only sharing a room, but also an impromptu kiss. A kiss which had been a whole lot hotter than I'd bargained for.

When was the last time I'd taken the time to kiss a woman? Sadly, I couldn't remember. Instead, everything for the last few years had been about the "performance" for the club and what others would enjoy watching.

The elevator kiss had been a performance too. Which is what I repeated to myself over and over in order to keep the front of my jeans from making it obvious there'd been nothing fake about it. Especially the soft little moan which had me wanting to take her against the wall. What the fuck had I been thinking to take a taste when I now had to deny myself anything further?

I had to stifle a groan when my eyes fell upon her swollen lips.

Gauging my unexpected roommate's expression, I

decided she was still stunned. Whether it was from the scene downstairs or our kiss, I wasn't sure. Shawn's words about her being slow to put out gave me pause. What if I'd gone too far in the elevator by suggesting she kiss me? It had been petty to pull that stunt, but there was no forgetting the taste of her lips.

"Let me call downstairs about switching to a room with two beds." I'd rectify the situation right now. However, two minutes later, after the front desk clerk had checked and re-checked, it appeared we were out of luck. No alternate rooms were available.

"They don't have any double-bed rooms available, but they'll call me if one opens up. I can take the couch." The one half my size and which looked stiff as a board.

A smile pulled from her lips. "I'd like to see you fit on that thing. It's okay, Max, I can take the couch, or we can build a pillow wall between us on the bed if you're worried."

Now it was my turn to grin. "Worried about what, exactly?"

A pretty blush stained her cheeks. "I meant you seem to be the one concerned."

"I'm trying to be a gentleman."

She took a seat on the ornamental love seat. The cushion didn't squish at all, proving my assessment of its lack of comfort.

"I appreciate it, but I'm the one imposing on you. The last thing I'd do is take your bed."

There was a sadness to her, as if all of the adrenaline had run its course. Crossing over to where she sat, I took the chair across from her, our knees almost touching. My fingers lifted her chin until she had no choice but to focus on me.

"You all right?"

She swallowed hard. "Yeah. Thanks for allowing me a moment of triumph after Shawn's shitty comment."

"Tell me more about the prick. What does he do? Where did you meet?" I justified wanting to know everything as acting in the role of protective big brother. Honestly, I was interested in what had drawn her to a guy like him in the first place.

"He went to college with Tim and recently moved to New York City. He works for an investment company—Marquis Investments, I think he called it—as a financial advisor. He seemed like a nice guy from what Kate told me, so I agreed to meet for a blind date. Then we went on two other dates. I should've trusted my gut when it came to him, though. I knew something seemed off, like he was a fake, but I never expected such hostility. Once again, you saved me. Thank you."

"It was nothing." Lie of the century. I dropped my hand, filing the information on Shawn away in my brain. Especially where he worked. I happened to know the owner of the company. He was not only a patron of the club, but also handled investments for both Shane and me. "If it wouldn't hurt my sister's feelings, I'd tell you to hop in my SUV right now, and we'd be out of here."

She bestowed a smile on me, making my chest tight. "You'd drive me straight to the Philly cheesesteak street vendor and truly become my all-time favorite hero."

"There's also a chicken shawarma stand which is my Friday night stop." Crap, I hadn't meant it as an invitation. Thankfully, she didn't seem to think of it as such.

Her phone vibrated in her purse, causing her to check it. "Cocktails downstairs in thirty minutes."

"Will you be okay dealing with Shawn this entire weekend?"

She sighed. "Yeah, I'll ignore him, and it'll be fine. This is Kate's weekend. and I won't spoil anything by making it about me."

Something for me to remember too. If Oakley could put on a brave face for this weekend and deal with Shawn, then I could do the same and deal with seeing my parents.

A half hour later, she left for the cocktail hour downstairs. Although I was also invited, I was in no hurry to join. The less time I spent with my family, the more likelihood there'd be no drama.

But I'd also needed a minute to myself after seeing Oakley changed into skinny jeans and a black top. The new outfit accented all of her incredible curves. Long legs, an incredible ass, and breasts which practically begged for my mouth on them.

I blew out a breath. Damn. Being attracted to a woman was nothing new. Not acting on the attraction, however, definitely was.

Sending a quick text to Shane to see how things were going at the club brought a predictable response. He responded with an *all is good* and to enjoy the weekend. Dammit. I could use a club emergency about now. When another text came in, I expected it to be Shane again, but instead it was my sister, Kate.

"Get your butt down here and hug the bride-to-be."

Oh, boy. How did one ignore a text like that? You didn't. Time to suck it up. I showered quickly, and after changing into dark jeans and a forest-green button-down, I traded my Nikes for leather dress shoes. I might not be much on fashion, but as a club owner who was often visible, either behind the bar or on the floor, I knew how to dress well.

Once I stepped off the elevator onto the lobby floor, I took a deep breath to fight my nerves. How ironic to feel more anxious about seeing my family than about performing sexual acts naked in front of strangers.

All trepidation was replaced with genuine joy, however, when Kate spotted me across the bar and came running up to tackle hug me. For a small girl, she had enough power to nearly knock me over.

"Jesus, have you been prepping for your wedding or the strong man competition?"

She grinned. With her sleek brown hair cut in a bob and her big, blue eyes, she looked so much like our mom. "Ha. I'm so glad you're here, Max."

I smiled. "Me too, kiddo." My eyes left hers to survey the people in the bar.

"Don't worry. Mom and Dad aren't coming tonight. Just the bridal party and a few other friends. Come on."

She took my hand and dragged me over to the bar where I shook her fiancé's hand. "Nice to see you again, Tim." I'd met him when they'd dated as teenagers, and again in New York City a couple years ago when they'd been visiting, so it had been a while.

"You too." He looked adoringly at my sister.

Tim seemed like a decent guy with the exception of his choice of friends, if Shawn the asshole was any indication. He and my sister had been dating since high school, and although I couldn't understand marrying the first person you'd ever been with, it seemed to work for them. I was sure in a couple years' time I'd be an uncle.

A pang suddenly hit me over never being a part of Christmas. Although I'd never wanted children of my own, I would have enjoyed being the doting uncle who came home for holidays and spoiled them.

"Oh, and you remember Oakley? My best friend in the

whole entire world, joined at the hip all through middle and high school."

My lips twitched at the sight of her. Her hair was pulled into a sleek ponytail practically begging for me to wrap it around my fist. If she had any idea of the things I'd love to do to her, I was sure she'd run far, far away.

We hadn't discussed how to play this in front of my sister or what to tell people—especially given Shawn could've already told everyone about our elevator kiss. I decided to take my cue from her.

"Nice to see you again, Max."

"Nice to see you again too."

Her eyes twinkled. "How was the drive in?"

Damn, I could detect the smell of her lavender shampoo even from two feet away. "Unexpectedly good. Yours?"

"Same."

My quick scan of the bar didn't turn up any sign of Shawn. Perhaps the threat I'd whispered in his ear about staying the fuck away from her had worked.

"Let me get you a drink, Max," Kate offered. She went off to the bar with her fiancé, leaving me alone with Oakley.

"No drama with Shawn, I take it?" My sister didn't seem to know anything.

"Not so far. Evidently he's upstairs in his room working on a project he didn't finish for work. I told Kate I decided to get my own room because I wanted to take things slower."

"Take things slower how?" I wasn't being glib; I was truly baffled.

"Slower in the sense of not yet ready to sleep together."

Both my brows jumped up. She hadn't slept with Shawn? Immediately, I felt abashed for assuming she would have. Just because I hopped in bed with women to perform in front of others didn't mean other people didn't take the time to get to know someone first.

Another reason why she was off-limits. She wanted to be courted and start a relationship, not have a tawdry, no-strings weekend with a sex club owner. "I bet."

"Anyhow, my job as maid of honor is to ensure Kate has no wedding drama."

"In that case, you should send me home. Stat."

Her husky laughter made my entire body take notice. "Nice try. Oh, and I did get on the waiting list for a room in case there's a cancellation."

"It's not necessary. I would suggest we not advertise our arrangement to my sister to avoid damage to your reputation, but I'm guessing Shawn might spill the beans anyway."

She cocked her head to the side. "Why would you worry about my reputation?"

I lifted a brow. "My father hates my guts. I'm sure my sister has already had to deal with enough flack from my parents when she invited me to her wedding, but if they were to find out you're staying with me—? Well, let's just say I don't want their contempt for me to rub off on you."

She wrinkled her cute little nose as if the thought hadn't once occurred to her. Before she could respond, Kate returned with a bourbon for me.

"Thank you," I said turning my focus on my sister.

"You're welcome. Come on, I want to introduce you to the rest of the wedding party."

"Lead the way."

Chapter Seven

OAKLEY

It was impossible not to stare at Max as his sister introduced him to the other members of the wedding party across the room from me. Most of them he'd known years ago in school, but he hadn't seen any of them in over a decade. Although I knew he was uncomfortable being here, you couldn't tell from his charismatic manner.

I wondered about his comment regarding besmirching my reputation. Yes, I'd once been close with his family, but I certainly wouldn't pick a team as if there was a good and bad side. His remark made me even more curious about what had caused their falling out.

Over the course of the next couple hours, our group grabbed some tables, ordered some appetizers, and had a few more drinks. Despite Max being on the other side of the table, I couldn't keep my gaze off of him. He looked over at me a few times throughout the evening, as if he was silently saying, "I've got this."

Once the happy couple headed upstairs, I visited the ladies' room at the back of the bar before intending to call it a night. As I stepped out, the one person I hoped not to see was standing in the hall.

"You know Max is gay, right?" Shawn asserted.

I rolled my eyes.

"Your stunt in the elevator was pathetic."

I didn't bother to answer Shawn's comment. Instead, I moved to walk past him, but he grabbed my arm, making me hiss.

"Think about it. Choice of lifestyle caused him to be disowned by his parents, so it makes sense. Kate is the one who told Tim."

News to me, but even if it was true, how sad that Max's parents had cut off their child for his sexual orientation. It made me angry to think they'd be so narrow-minded.

I jerked my arm away. "I'm not sure why you think I'd care."

"Because you're practically in heat around him."

"You're a pig. So glad you turned into a psycho on the highway, so I could find out earlier rather than later. By the way, don't you have some work to do for your office? You know, the work you should've finished before leaving town?"

Direct hit judging by the way his face turned red. He returned fire. "You know, Kate had some interesting things to say about why you and your ex broke up."

Whoosh. Blood rushed to my ears in a roar. No. She wouldn't have betrayed me by telling Shawn about the video. But his next words proved I was wrong.

"That's right. I know all about your sex video. The only reason I put up with our bullshit dates and waiting to sleep together was the hope of getting my own little souvenir."

I stepped back as if he'd struck me, my stomach turning and the bile rising to my throat. The sharp impact of my best friend's betrayal in telling him made it tough to breathe.

"No one would want a video with you in it, Scott."

The sound of Max's voice and his footsteps moving closer caused goose bumps on my arms. A possessive hand landed on my hip.

Shawn's face turned an even deeper shade of red, anger flashing in his eyes when Max deliberately slipped up on his name.

I started to shake, but Max's arm pulled me into him, and the heat of his body warmed me up from the chill running through me.

"You know, a real man understands what a woman needs. But you were never that man, were you, Steve?"

Emboldened by Max's words, I took it a step further. "Thank goodness you left me on the side of the road so I could find one. Ready to go upstairs, Max?"

I was feeling brave until he spun me around to face him. Much to my relief, Max didn't mind the ruse I'd implicitly proposed. His gaze heated as it collided with mine. I swallowed hard, needing to remember for a moment this wasn't real. My body wasn't getting the memo, however.

"Does Kate know about you slumming it with her brother?" Shawn asked, snapping me out of it.

He could tell the world as far as I was concerned. But Max wasn't having it. "Does your boss at Marquis Investments know he has a prick for an employee? Small world, Shawny boy. I know the owner, Edward Lincoln, very well."

Shawn's entire face blanched.

"So what I said earlier about you staying the fuck away from Oakley comes with an addendum: keep your mouth shut. Otherwise, not only do your college friends, including the groom, find out what an asshole you are, but your boss gets an earful too. Hard to keep up a lease payment on a new BMW without a job."

Damn. Max definitely had his number. Shawn opened and closed his mouth before stomping away.

"Well, then," I quipped, amusement lacing my words. "Keeping that little tidbit of leverage under wraps, huh? Do you really know the owner?"

He chuckled. "I do. The lease on the car was a lucky guess."

I grinned in triumph. "Thanks for the assist once again." It was almost enough to make me forget about the sex video.

He cupped my chin, looking for a moment as if he'd lean down and kiss me.

My heart threatened to beat out of my chest. Was it possible to find a man who didn't think my video made me a whore? Who didn't judge me for it? But just as my hopes started to rise, they dropped sharply along with his hand.

"I need to check in with work."

Disappointment lanced through me, but I forced a smile. Maybe Max was gay. Or perhaps he simply wasn't into me. "I'll let you get to it. Thanks again. Have a good night."

I went straight up to the room. Once there, I changed into shorts and a T-shirt, washed my face, brushed my teeth, and grabbed an extra blanket and pillow from the closet. I'd settled onto the most uncomfortable love seat in the world when the distinct sound of Max's keycard sounded in the door. In an attempt to make sharing a room less awkward than the earlier portion of the evening, I feigned sleep, breathing a sigh of relief when he went straight into the bathroom, closed the door, and ran the water.

The door opened, the light turned off, and the bedspread rustled, causing my heart to beat faster. Once his footsteps came toward me, I squeezed my eyes shut harder, but to no avail.

"I know you're awake, Oakley."

"No, you don't," I quipped unable to help myself. His chuckle made me smile.

"Come get in the bed."

"No, thanks. I'm very comfortable right here." Considering the way my sex fantasy had been manifesting itself at night and my attraction to Max, I couldn't take a chance on waking up in the middle of the night to find myself dry humping his leg. Nope, I'd stay right here in the safety zone.

"There's no way that thing is comfortable."

It really wasn't, but it beat the hell out of humiliating myself in front of him yet again. I fluffed up the pillow. "It's fine."

"What's sticking out from under the cushion?"

Nope. I wouldn't fall for it. "Nice try."

He turned on the table lamp. "I'm serious. Are those your panties?"

I bolted upright. "Of course not." But much to my horror, there was indeed a scrap of lace peeking out from under the cushion beneath me.

Ew. Unable to believe there was a pair of underwear lodged under the pillow, I pinched the edge of the fabric and pulled, hoping to prove him wrong. A stranger's black thong was my reward.

"Oh my God, that's disgusting." I dropped the offending article into the trash and ran into the bathroom. There I scrubbed like a surgeon from hand to elbow.

Max's laughter followed me. "Why on earth would anyone choose the most uncomfortable mini couch to have sex on?"

I walked back out, thoroughly repulsed. "No kidding."

Max was still grinning, a twinkle in his eye. "Obviously, you don't want to sleep on the 'sex couch' now."

God, I really didn't.

He stepped toward the bed, a smirk on his face as he patted the mattress. "Take your pick. Sleep on the sex sofa or come to the safety of the no-sex bed."

Chapter Eight

MAX

There was no way I was letting her sleep on the uncomfortable half-couch. The sex sofa had given me all the ammunition I needed to convince her. "Get in the bed, Oakley."

I used sheer willpower to avoid staring at her perky chest in the tight T-shirt and her shapely legs in those boy shorts. It was benign as far as nightwear went, and yet I'd never seen such clothing look sexier on a woman. She had an incredible body. Small frame, perky tits, curvy hips, and a runner's legs, long and lean.

She sighed but ultimately went to one side of the bed and pulled down the comforter.

Content I'd won the battle, I turned out the light by the couch. I couldn't remember the last time I'd spent the night in a bed with a woman, especially in a platonic way. I undressed down to my boxers before getting into bed. Even by moonlight, I didn't miss the look of appreciation she gave me. I wasn't vain about my body, but I worked out and kept in shape.

A huff left her lips, and she grabbed two pillows from her

side and put them down the middle of the bed.

"You don't trust me?" Though I was attracted to her, she sure as hell didn't have to worry about me making unwanted advances.

"The pillow wall is for your sake, not mine." She huddled down under the comforter, secure on her side of the bed.

"What are you talking about?"

"I don't want to accidentally—you know."

A chuckle rumbled in my chest, and I turned to face her great wall of fluff. "I don't know. Please tell me more about what you think might happen if we were not to have these two safety pillows between us." I removed a pillow so I could see her face. The pale light only made her more beautiful.

Her gaze hit mine, and I swear I could feel my heart beating out loud. When was the last time I'd had this sort of pull toward a woman?

"What are you afraid you might accidentally do?" I was fascinated and more than a little turned on.

She shook her head. "Forget it."

She was suddenly shy and unlike the type of woman I was used to. I replaced the pillow. "Safety wall is engaged. Now you can tell me."

She giggled. "Like a confessional?"

"Yes. Now, tell me how you think you'll sin, my child." It would be helpful if I could conjure up a picture of her as a kid right about now.

"Sometimes I naturally seek out the heat in the bed."

"You're worried you'll—what? Cuddle me?"

"Mm-hm."

A cuddle sounded both incredible and like torture.

The sound of a soft yawn came from the other side of the pillow. "Thanks for rescuing me from the sex couch, Max."

My smile was wide. "Anytime. Get some sleep."

I stirred in my slumber, waking to the sound of heavy breathing. It took me a moment to remember where I was and that Oakley was on the other side of the fluffy mountain. Like a creeper, I couldn't resist moving the pillow in front of me so I could see her face.

She was the picture of beauty and innocence, her hair splayed out on the white sheets. It was times like this I struggled with my life choices. The harsh reality was I could never have a woman like Oakley. She deserved to find a man who could give her a future, the kind which included a house in the suburbs—probably next to my sister—kids, a minivan, and weekends spent doing family things like soccer and YMCA shit. Not a guy who worked at a sex club with few weekends off, who didn't want kids, and who wasn't even sure he was capable of a meaningful romantic relationship.

Replacing the pillow, I turned and scrubbed my hands over my face.

I rolled onto my side, ready to get back to sleep when a gasp had me turning toward Oakley. I was about to check on her when a low moan put my entire body on notice.

Chapter Nine

OAKLEY

The erotic setting was familiar. Only this time, my eyes weren't covered with a blindfold. Instead, my gaze was fixated on the man kissing the inside of my thighs. His sandy hair was familiar. I trusted this man. I knew this man. He focused on my clit, making me gasp at the contact. Two fingers moved deep inside of me, causing me to moan. He looked up with a devilish grin I'd know anywhere.

Max.

"Oakley." His voice penetrated my fading dream. It was husky, sexy, but out of place in the scene.

"Wake up, sweetheart."

"Huh?" My eyes flew open to see the face from my dreams bathed in the moonlight.

"I think you were having a nightmare."

Definitely wasn't a nightmare, but this certainly felt like the start to one.

He turned on the bedside lamp and sat up, his gaze fixed on me. I noticed the moment he realized where my hand was. It was a beat before I did.

Frack. I removed it quickly, realizing too late my fingers

were coated with my arousal. I moved to hide the evidence but not before he grabbed my wrist.

"Don't."

"Don't what?" My whisper was barely audible. This was the point where he should be turning red, and I should be humiliated. Instead, the heat of his gaze made my body shake.

"Don't be embarrassed. It's hot as fuck."

I blamed my blurted-out thought on the fact I no longer had brain cells accessible. "You're not gay?"

Instead of being offended, he chuckled. "Is that the rumor?"

"Yes, I mean it was mentioned." I watched, transfixed, as he took one of my fingers between his lips.

"Would a gay man enjoy the taste of your pussy?"

I guessed the answer was no, but fuck if I could have said anything right then. The feel of his tongue swiping my taste from my finger put me on the edge of an orgasm. "I think I'm dreaming," I muttered, closing my eyes and reopening them to test the theory.

"The dream might belong to me. I told myself I wouldn't touch you." He suddenly released my hand with an expression akin to torment.

I was confused. How did we go from something so unbelievably hot to not? "You don't want to touch me?"

He ran a hand through his hair. "You're my sister's best friend and looking for something I can't offer."

"You can't offer great sex?"

He sucked in a sharp breath, his expression conflicted. Then he leaned over and flicked off the light. "Let's get some sleep."

Stunned, I felt tears spring to my eyes. Rejection was hard to swallow. I'd been better off believing he was gay. In addition to my humiliation, my body remained on edge. I knew if

I ignored it, it would rebel against me and take over my dreams again. Which left one solution. I moved to get out of the bed and take things into the shower.

Max's voice stopped me. "Don't you dare."

"Dare what?"

"Don't you dare finish yourself off."

Irritation sparked my temper. "Unlike you, I'm not about to deny myself."

"Do it here."

I couldn't have heard him correctly.

"Masturbate beside me. Let me listen to you come."

It was the hottest thing I'd ever heard. I was officially speechless. I wasted no time, already touching myself as I climbed back into the bed. I was wet, so much so the sound became obvious in the silence of the room. His muttered curses on the other side of the ridiculous pillow wall fueled me. It was the ultimate foreplay for my fantasy.

"I'm so turned on," I whispered. The dark room and barrier emboldened me to share.

"Fuck, so am I."

A thought popped into my head. "Are you touching yourself, Max?"

He huffed out a breath, seemingly hesitant to share. "Yeah."

Confidence bloomed in my chest. "Do you wish it was you touching me right now?"

"God, yes."

"I was dreaming about you." I couldn't believe I was confessing the truth. Perhaps the bed really was a confessional.

"Tell me about the dream." His breathing was labored.

"My hands are tied, and I'm on my back. You're kissing my thighs, and your fingers are inside of me." I returned to my fantasy, but this time I was awake and sharing the details with another person. "I'm close." My legs shook, and my muscles went taut.

"Fuck, I need for you to come for me, Oakley."

My climax hit me like a wave, and I cried out at the release. It wasn't until I started to recover that I remembered he'd been listening to it all. Perhaps if I lay still long enough, he'd ignore me and not say anything.

"Oakley?"

I squeezed my eyes shut in shame. I'd confessed too much. Gone too far in sharing my secret thoughts.

"Talk to me, beautiful."

"I'm too embarrassed." It was as if my recurring dream and sexual fantasies had somehow gotten locked inside the wrong person.

"I don't know why. Listening to you was the most unexpectedly hot thing I've done in, maybe, ever."

"Really?"

He moved the top pillow so he could look at me.

"Absolutely."

"Then why are you so reluctant to touch me?"

"There are a lot of reasons, but the biggest is you waited three dates and still hadn't slept with Shawn, so it's clear sex is not something you treat casually."

"It wasn't the sex I was waiting for. It was the comfort and trust. And after three dates, I wasn't getting it from Shawn. I have both with you."

He looked conflicted, but then smirked. "Remember when I said this bed was a no-sex bed?"

My lips tipped up in a smile. "I do."

"I lied. I need more of you."

My head nodded. I think from this point forward, I'd only nod yes with this man.

Max moved quickly to toss both pillows onto the floor and pulled me into the center of the bed. Next, he tugged down my boy shorts.

"Take off your T-shirt, beautiful. I need you naked."

I was thankful he left the lights off. The moonlight was softer. My body shivered at the way he was so focused on me. The way his voice betrayed his need. As soon as my shirt was gone, he hooked my thong with both thumbs and slid it down my legs. He held the lacy scrap in his hands, the significance not dawning on me until he reached up and bound my hands with it. Fuck. He'd not only tied me up with my thong, he'd also recreated the details I'd given him from my dream. I was ready to combust on the spot.

His eyes locked on mine. Although he was still wearing his boxers, I'd glimpsed the outline of his erection. "Did you finish before?" It occurred to me I hadn't bothered to ask yet, being so caught up in my own orgasm.

He glanced up, the dimples in full effect. "Not yet. Plenty of time."

I was about to ask another question, but all thought ceased once his mouth descended. His tongue ran my length. Another orgasm wasn't his goal, however. Not yet. Instead he lapped up the evidence of my last one first as if he couldn't help himself. He didn't start with one finger, but with three entering me slowly.

"Squeeze me."

I did as he asked, loving the hiss of his breath at the action. As soon as I relaxed again, he went to work, curling his fingers up toward my outer wall while descending on my clit like a master of all things pussy. His tongue was diabolical.

I'd often thought a man had no real chance of living up to a vibrator when it came to clitoral stimulation, but I was proved oh, so wrong. Max wasn't like the previous boys I'd been with who licked around and hoped they hit the right spot. Nope, he lasered in like a pilot on a target. He might as well have delivered a bomb, he destroyed me so completely.

By the time I opened my eyes and recovered coherent thought, Max was up on his knees, watching me.

"How am I doing for a supposed gay man?" His fingers were still very much inside of me, languidly moving through my wetness.

"It wasn't me who thought you— Oh, God, that feels good." He pressed on my clit with his thumb while working his fingers inside of me.

"For the record, I'm not gay. Or bisexual, or been in the CIA undercover for the last ten years protecting my family by staying away."

I chuckled at the myriad of rumors he was concocting about why he'd broken with his parents. But then I voiced my earlier insecurity. "I thought maybe you weren't into me."

"I'm literally in you."

My eyes rolled at his bad joke.

Chapter Ten

MAX

The way Oakley climaxed was incredible. There was no pretense with her, no acting. Just pure, unfiltered reaction to the pleasure I'd given her body. It was intoxicating. It was enough for me to ignore all the reasons I'd given myself as to why she should stay off-limits.

She trusted me. She was comfortable with me. She wanted great sex.

"I thought maybe after hearing about the video, you would think less of me."

Her words were said on a whisper; the vulnerability hitting me square in the chest. My lips crashed to hers. I loved the way she moaned into my mouth when she tasted herself. As I pulled away, I untied her hands and held both of them in mine.

"I don't give a flying fuck about a video. The fact you trusted your ex-boyfriend and he went on to break your trust shows his true colors, not yours. Same with douchebag Shawn, who thinks it's appropriate to hang it over your head as if you should be wearing a scarlet letter. You have nothing to be ashamed of. Ever. Do you understand?"

She nodded, closing the gap and kissing me again. Fuck. Oakley was an incredible kisser. She dueled with her tongue and entwined her fingers in my hair like she craved me.

It occurred to me I was better at *do as I say* rather than *do as I do.* I still struggled with my own insecurity about owning the club and what I'd sacrificed in my life as a result. A sense of fair play made me think I should share my secret with Oakley. She'd said she trusted me, but could she actually trust me if I hadn't been completely honest with her?

But I didn't want to take a chance on wrecking the moment. And the way she was kissing my neck made it difficult to remember what I'd intended to say. When was the last time someone had wanted me for me? Max. Not Max at the club. Not Max the millionaire. No choreography, no props, just a woman who wanted me for me.

So I wouldn't tell her about the club. Not yet. However, another bout of conscience hit me: the reason I hadn't wanted to get involved with her in the first place. "I don't want to mislead you about what this is."

"Jesus," she muttered encircling her hand around my erection. Yeah, so I'd been blessed when it came to dick size.

"I apologize. I've been dick-zazzled, what did you say?"

I threw my head back with laughter. Fuck if I knew what I was going to say. More kissing, less talking seemed a better strategy. Nope. Think, Max, think. I managed to blurt out, "I'm not a relationship guy." Men who owned sex clubs didn't date nice girls from small towns who were looking for their future husband and a three-bedroom, two-bath rambler in the same neighborhood they'd grown up.

"Good. Been there, got the parting video, not interested in another one anytime soon."

I smiled against her lips as I took them again in a searing

kiss. "I'm being serious. This is only sex, and no feelings outside of friendship."

"'Kay." She grazed my ear with her lips.

I didn't think she comprehended the gravity of my words. The last thing I wanted was to hurt her. Or cause a falling out with my sister because Oakley thought there was something more going on between us. "I'm being serious."

She sat back, her expression amused. "Fine, I promise this is only for the weekend, and there will be no feelings. Will you promise the same?"

I chuckled, enjoying her sass after her earlier insecurity. "I promise. What happens in this room during this weekend stays in this room." We'd enjoy each other and part as friends on Sunday. Sounded like a reasonable plan.

"Good." She dove in for the kiss.

I could kiss her for days, but I also wanted to be inside of her. One big problem though. "I didn't bring condoms." I'd been so anxious about this weekend and seeing my family, it never once occurred to me to come prepared.

She broke the kiss, her eyes wide, and her lips tipping up in a grin. "Damn. This really is the no-sex bed."

My laughter came instantly. "Seems so." Perhaps the cockblocking gods of the world were sending a message.

"Would it be too petty to go ask Shawn for a condom? Isn't like he'll be using them."

Now we both laughed. I ignored the kernel of jealousy over the idea she could've been sleeping with him by now if he hadn't dumped her on the highway and shown his true colors.

"Perhaps. But I doubt we're the same size." It wasn't a brag, simply a fact.

"True." Her eyes traveled down to my boxers. My very

tented boxers. Pre-ejaculation seeped out at the sight of her licking her lips.

"Tell me what you want." I hardly recognized my own husky voice.

"I want to taste you."

Fuck. Although I had stamina in spades, I feared I might blow with the first touch. It had been too long, and I wanted Oakley too much to hold out for long.

"Tell me how you want it." I was normally the one to take charge, but tonight I wanted her to call the shots.

"Take off your boxers, then lie on the bed."

I did as I was told, wishing I could see her better in the dark room.

Her hand gripped around my cock, tentative at first, but growing bolder as she explored my length.

"Jesus, you're perfection," she murmured.

I couldn't respond because in the next instant, her lips had fastened on my crown. Little licks down my shaft to my base followed. I wasn't sure if her moves were practiced or exploratory, but it felt like torture in the very best way. My hands gripped the sheets, and I struggled not to make a fool of myself and come early.

"Baby, you're killing me."

She pushed me between her lips, humming.

The sensation caused my balls to draw up. "Oh, fuck."

She took me deep. Then again and again as she set a rhythm. I gritted my teeth, wanting to prolong the exquisite pleasure for as long as possible. But once her assault included sucking my balls into her mouth, I knew I was on borrowed time. I'd been hard over the last hour, I wouldn't last much longer. "I'm going to come."

She didn't let up, instead doubling down on her efforts.

"Fuuuuuuuck," I moaned, ejaculating long spurts into her mouth.

She swallowed like a pro, licking her lips as if what I gave her wasn't enough.

This beautiful woman had officially rocked my world.

Chapter Eleven

OAKLEY

The alarm on my phone woke me out of a deep sleep. After finding the offending device, I pressed the off button and rolled over to find Max's side of the bed empty. A glance toward the bathroom confirmed he'd left the room.

Flipping onto my back, I reveled in how well I slept after we'd participated in the oral Olympics. Never again would I date another twenty-something-year-old. Nope, only older men who knew what they were doing from now on. Max had also managed to lift a weight of shame off my chest about the video with my ex. He hadn't judged me for it.

We had this weekend. We'd promised to enjoy one another, but come Sunday when we went home, it would be over. I'd meant it when I said I wasn't looking for a relationship, but I'd be lying if I said a couple days would be enough time with him.

I started to get excited about the idea he might be downstairs in the giftshop buying condoms. But wait, did they even have condoms here? They had to, right? Like, Hotel 101: have condoms available in the gift shop.

Knowing I had no more time to dawdle, I dragged myself into the shower. The plans for today consisted of breakfast with the girls, a full-day spa treatment, and then the rehearsal followed by the rehearsal dinner tonight. By the time I was dressed and ready, still no Max. I fought my disappointment.

Wedding duties awaited.

MAX

The cold air burned my lungs, yet the outdoor run was exhilarating. Much better than the usual treadmill runs in my apartment. After I started out on the five-mile course I'd planned on my phone, I let my music relax my body and my mind go clear.

Yet as much as I fought it, the memory of Oakley took precedence. Fuck, she'd been so incredible. And having her body curled into me while she slept had done something to me.

I found myself picking up the pace, wanting nothing more than to wake her up with my tongue. After that, my mission was to drive into town and get condoms.

It wasn't easy to run with a semi-hard penis, so I turned around sooner than I'd intended and sprinted back. As I entered the front lobby, however, all other thoughts were doused when I spotted my mother at the front desk.

She was smaller than I remembered. Her jet-black hair was cut in the same blunt bob I'd always known, but it looked to be peppered with gray. When she turned, I noted a few more wrinkles, but my mother was still a beautiful woman. Her brows went high when she spotted me, and we both stood there as if in a trance.

I decided to go first. "Hi."

Tears came to her eyes. "Hi."

But as soon as hope started to grow we might enjoy a long-overdue hug, it quickly evaporated when she looked around like a scared rabbit. "I should go before your father comes in."

God forbid she go against my father's wishes and say hello to her baby boy. Here I'd thought I'd be prepared for seeing her. But it was like a fresh wound had been re-exposed. "Right, wouldn't want him knowing you'd said hi to your only son."

She wrung her hands. "You know that's not fair. You made choices."

"Yeah, well, so did you. Only difference is my choices didn't cut someone I supposedly loved from my life. Take care, Mother."

Pride propelled me past her and into the elevator. The saving grace was feeling too angry for tears. Once I was on my floor, I walked down the hallway toward my door, which I saw open and Oakley step out.

She was stunning, with her hair down and wearing a long, navy dress and a cream-colored sweater. She looked up, pure pleasure in her eyes at the sight of me.

The sensation of meeting someone who was happy to see me was indescribable.

"Hi, did you work out?"

"I did. Where are you heading?" My voice was gruff with the emotion of my encounter with my mom.

"Ladies' brunch downstairs." She regarded me closely. "Are you okay?"

Last thing she needed was my baggage. "Yeah, fine."

"No you're not. Come on." She took my hand and pulled me into the room. "What happened?"

I let out a long sigh. “I saw my mom.”

She swallowed hard. “How did it go?”

“She was afraid my father would catch her saying hello to me. I didn’t think it would—” I scrubbed a hand over my face, hating how vulnerable I sounded.

“Hurt so badly?” she finished.

I nodded, not trusting myself to speak.

“I’m sorry, Max. I can’t even imagine how difficult this is for you to be here.”

I loathed the sympathy on her face and in her voice. Time to snap out of it. “It’s fine. You should go, or you’ll be late.”

She looked torn.

“Really, go. You look beautiful, by the way.”

Her pretty blush was already improving my mood. “Thank you. How was the workout?”

“I went for a run. Cut off two miles of my planned five with thoughts of waking you up. Sorry I was late.”

“Oh, yeah, what did you have in mind?”

My hands framed her face. “You’ll find out tonight. Now go before I ruin all your makeup.”

She shivered before moving forward and taking my lips. The kiss was slow, intimate, and everything I didn’t know I needed. “The day cannot go by fast enough.”

“No, it can’t.”

After a hot shower, and dressing in warm clothes, I left the hotel behind and drove the eight miles into the heart of my home town. It looked much the same. Like a beacon, Fran and Dan’s Diner called to me, still located at the end of Main Street. The parking lot was packed, which didn’t surprise me given how good their breakfast was. I could practically taste the bacon breakfast burrito I used to order every time I came here as a teenager.

Walking in was a stroll down memory lane with the

chrome and Formica countertop, the red stools, and the old-time pleather booths with the mini jukeboxes on the table. I wondered if they still played music after all these years. Fran and Dan had long been friends and neighbors to my parents. Although they didn't have children of their own, they'd never minded letting us kids come over to use their pool during the summers.

There was an open spot at the counter, and I'd shrugged out of my coat when doubt unexpectedly hit me. What if Fran's reaction was like my mother's? I wasn't sure I could bear it. Deciding not to take the chance, I turned to go, but someone called my name.

"Max?"

I'd recognize that voice anywhere. Pivoting, I saw the bright red hair and the even brighter smile. "Hi, Fran."

She was built like a brick house, and yet she moved like a woman possessed. I braced myself for the hug.

"It is you. Oh my God. I was hoping you'd come home for your sister's wedding. How are you, sweetie?"

"I'm good. Thank you."

She took a step back, knowing no boundaries when it came to squeezing my arms and patting my chest. "You've grown." She pinched my cheek. "And so very handsome. Come on, take a seat. Let's get you some food. Bacon burrito, side of bacon, right?"

"You got it." It was something to know she remembered after all these years.

She bustled around the counter, pouring me a coffee while I took a seat. I couldn't help wincing when she shouted toward the kitchen. "Dan, get your butt out here."

The old man shouted back. "Keep your knickers on, woman."

He came through the swinging door looking more

stooped than the last time I'd seen him, but still just as skinny and frail. To tell the truth, I hadn't been sure he'd still be around considering he was a chain-smoking, whiskey-drinking, watching-your-cholesterol-is-for-pussies kind of guy. "What do you want, woman? I'm busy makin' bacon."

Their love language made me chuckle. I hadn't understood it when I was younger, but now I appreciated fully.

Fran had one hand on her hip and gestured toward me with the other. "Right there."

Squinting his eyes at me, Dan took his glasses out of his pocket, making me wonder how the hell he cooked if they weren't on his face. "Maxamillion?"

Only he'd ever used the nickname. "Yes, sir."

He flashed a dentured grin, one of ten I'd ever seen come from the man. "Come around here, boy, and give these old bones a squeeze."

I did as he asked, careful not to squeeze too hard. "Good to see you."

"You too. Boy, did you end up big. What can I get you? Bacon burrito with a side of bacon?"

"I've been dreaming about it."

He scoffed but gave me another smile. "Coming right up."

Fran put a glass of OJ next to my coffee. "You see your folks?"

The question was expected, but it didn't make my reply any easier. "Saw my mom this morning. Nothing has changed."

She tsked. "Never made any sense to me. Knew your dad always had a stick up his ass about you becoming an attorney and going into practice with him, and he'd always been a self-righteous son of a bitch when it came to his way or the highway, but never thought they'd disown their only son for owning a club that doesn't suit their tastes."

Orange juice went down the wrong pipe. Her meaty fist pounded between my shoulders until I could breathe again. "I'm okay. Thanks."

"You didn't think we knew? Your mom used to be my best friend."

"Used to be?"

She smiled sadly. "We still talk from time to time, neighborly, but I lost all respect for her the moment she went along with your father in not talking to you. I regret we didn't stay in touch with you, but please know we were always on your side. Although Dan and I don't use the Internet or the words on the phones, we're always here."

"I'm sorry, Fran. I never meant for our fallout to affect you and Dan."

Her hand covered mine. "Don't you dare apologize. It was a long time coming. Your father didn't much like your mother hanging out with me anyhow."

My father had always been tough on me and expected perfection, which for him translated into doing what he said without question. But my mother had been the softness to even it out. I'd always considered myself a mama's boy until the point she decided to quit loving me.

As if Fran could read my mind, she said, "Didn't come without a steep cost. There's a heaviness weighing on her ever since things happened."

I wasn't sure that made me feel any better about it. But my father had always ruled with a heavy hand, which included expecting his wife to agree with him in all things.

"You know, I always thought your father cut you off more because you dared defy him rather than because he had a problem with the club. But of course, he used self-righteous bullshit to justify it all. Part of me thinks he kept waiting for you to fail and come home with your tail between your legs, so he could tell you I told you so. You doing well just pissed him off further."

I often thought the same. Yes, my parents went to church, and my father was socially conservative, but he seemed to apply his views as he saw fit rather than according to any ideology. Hell, I could remember my dad encouraging me to "hit it" with every cheerleader I could in order to sow my wild oats in high school. So why now was there such shame over what I'd chosen to do? And more importantly, why did I let it affect me, even a decade later?

"Will you be at the wedding?" I asked Fran.

"Wouldn't miss it. Kate ensured we would attend by coming in here to hand deliver the invitation. I even bought a dress and got Dan's old suit cleaned for the occasion."

"I'd love to sit with you both."

"And we'd love to sit with you. Let me check on your food, honey."

Chapter Twelve

OAKLEY

I hadn't wanted to leave Max up in the room alone. Although I wasn't close with my parents, I couldn't imagine not being able to pick up the phone to call either one of them if I was upset, happy, or simply missed them. They might have established new lives without me since the divorce, but I knew either one of them would be on a plane in a heartbeat if I really needed them. Max's mother wouldn't even hug him.

I eyed his mom over the breakfast table in the hotel restaurant, sensing a sadness about her. Max's father had always been a hard man who loved to hear himself talk, but his mother had been warm, friendly, and always about her two kids. But she'd changed.

Kate slid into the seat beside me. "Hey, what's up with you and Shawn? Someone said he was angry with you last night."

I let out a breath. Since she'd brought it up, perhaps it was best to tell her the truth. "I wanted to wait until after the weekend to tell you this, but—

She held up her hand. "No, no, no. I don't want to hear it. You two need to get along for this wedding. I mean it. Work out your problems, so I don't have to deal with them. I have enough happening with my own family. I don't want to deal with any more drama, so figure out how to get along. Apologize."

"Apologize for what?"

"For whatever it takes to keep the peace. And don't ask me to set you up again with anyone."

I didn't remember having asked in the first place. Now I wondered if Shawn had been telling the truth about doing Kate a favor in asking me out.

But I held my tongue. It was clear she didn't want to hear it. Our friendship was feeling the strain. It wouldn't surprise me if we ended up doing no more than exchanging yearly holiday cards and occasional Facebook posts in the coming years. Meanwhile, I had to get through this weekend.

"We'll get along. Best behavior, I promise."

"Good. Are you excited about going to the spa?" she asked, changing the subject.

"You bet." At least I wouldn't have to see Shawn there.

At the spa, I opted for a simple manicure, not having a lot of extra cash to spend on extravagant treatments. Afterward, I simply had fun hanging out with Kate and our other friends. Between the spa and the rehearsal, I'd hoped to see Max up in the room, but he wasn't in sight. After changing over into my black cocktail dress, I went downstairs to catch a ride to the church with the three other bridesmaids.

My day had been great up until the point I had to deal with Shawn again at the church. I scrutinized his over-gelled hair, over-bleached teeth, and brand-name trousers, which were too tight around his thighs. How had I thought he was attractive? Perhaps once someone showed how ugly they were on the inside, there was no hiding it on the outside.

"Hey, slut," he whispered sidling up so only I could hear him.

I didn't bother to turn toward him. Thankfully, Max had given me new confidence when it came to dealing with assholes like Shawn. "Is a woman a slut when she doesn't sleep with you? I'm so confused by the slut-shaming rules these days."

"Where's your boy toy? Did he get tired of faking things with you for my benefit?"

"Man, I can't keep up. First, I'm a slut. Then I'm not sleeping with you or him? So hard to keep track. As for Max, there's nothing fake about him." I let the innuendo drop though I knew it was childish to stoop to Shawn's level.

"I'm sure the men he fucks enjoy it," he snarled.

I pivoted so I could make eye contact. "Why, Shawn, you sound almost too defensive. Almost like you've been entertaining some deep-seated fantasies. Is that what this is all about? You're jealous because Max is more into me than you?"

My words had their desired effect when his entire face turned red, making me think I couldn't be entirely off base. "Shut up."

"No, you shut up. At least for the next two days. You will play nice and make Kate think we're getting along. Otherwise, I'll tell Max to call your boss. And since he's probably already unhappy with your work based on your phone call yesterday, I'm assuming Max's additional information might not go over well. Do you understand?"

I could practically hear his teeth grinding. Among other things, Shawn was a poor loser. "Fine."

He remained civil for the rest of the rehearsal, if you

could call pouting and giving me the cold shoulder well-mannered. Keeping up my fake smiles had been torture, but by the end of the rehearsal, I could call my performance a success.

We had a few minutes after returning to the hotel before dinner, allowing me time to run up to the room. Upon entering, I was treated to the sight of Max dressed up in a well-tailored suit. He was using the wall mirror to put on his tie.

I whistled low. "Looking good."

He turned with a grin. His smile soon faded as he surveyed me from head to toe, his expression giving me goose bumps and taking up the temperature in the room several degrees. "You look incredible. Did Shawn behave at the church?"

My immediate frown must've clued him in.

"I'm going to—"

"No, no, you're not. I can fight my own battles." The last thing Max needed was any more problems this weekend. He had enough going on with his parents. Not only that, but judging by my last conversation with Kate, I'd be the one blamed for any drama.

"Here, let me help." I walked over and took hold of his tie, loving the excuse to be close to him. His cologne smelled divine. Masculine and fresh, it made me want to shove my face into his shirt and breathe deep.

"How much time do we have?" he asked huskily.

I groaned at the unfairness of it all. "Not enough. I have pictures in five minutes."

He peppered my neck with kisses, making my entire body shiver. "We'll have plenty of time tonight."

"Does that mean you went shopping?"

"Big box by the bed."

My glance zeroed in on the large box of condoms on the nightstand. "How many do you think we'll need?"

"Mm. Depends on how you feel about walking tomorrow."

Good Lord. It was going to be a very long dinner.

Chapter Thirteen

MAX

I'd dreaded this evening all day long. I'd even gone so far as to text my sister, hoping she'd tell me she didn't want me attending the dinner after all. No such luck. But then Oakley had walked in, and my night took a turn for the better.

"I need something before I go," she said, framing my face.

"Name it."

"This." She pressed her lips against mine, slipping her tongue inside my mouth and making me want to ravish her on the spot.

"You'll ruin your lipstick."

"I don't care."

Jesus, she was addictive. "We'd better go before I tie you up and make you late."

The way her eyes blazed revealed how much the idea turned her on.

"You and I need to have a talk about your fantasies. I want to hear all of them." My words had the desired effect when she shivered, but then she averted her eyes.

Shit, I'd pushed her too hard. Tying her up with her panties last night had been hot as hell. It was a pretty soft kink in my view, but it had probably been a big step for her. Her reaction now reconfirmed my view that although we'd enjoy this weekend together, she'd never fit into my world. The thought made me unexpectedly sad. "We'd better go."

It wasn't until we were on the elevator together I realized we should've staggered our entrances. "Maybe you should go in first."

She rolled her eyes. "There will be a lot of people entering the restaurant. You and I walking in together won't be a big deal."

I hoped she was right.

OAKLEY

Assigned seats. Dammit, I was placed next to Shawn. He sat there with a smirk, my misery making him happy.

"I'll trade you." Max snatched up my place card and grinned at Shawn, his new neighbor. "Go ahead and sit across from us, Oakley."

"Do you always do what he tells you?" Shawn sniped.

"I do when it benefits me. And when it comes to Max, a lot does." I hadn't meant to make the words sound dirty, but I'd clearly hit that mark judging by the way Shawn flushed and Max chuckled.

My lips twitched when I took my seat across from both men. The comparison between them was startling. I was looking at a man versus a spoiled frat boy. Max's shoulders took up more than the width of his chair; his manners were refined and relaxed. Meanwhile, Shawn was in full-pout mode. When Max winked at me, I had to bring up my hand to cover my laughter.

Dinner was a mundane affair. Kate and Tim were seated at the head of the table along with their parents. I noticed Tim's siblings were seated up there too. Once again, I felt a pang for how Max must feel to be left out of his own family.

The food was delicious, the wine even better. Seated next to me, Nancy, a girl I'd gone to high school with, was super chatty. After a few glasses of wine, she chose to address Max. "Why is it you haven't been home in years? Kate never said."

I could see him visibly tense. "I get very busy with work."

Shawn's eyes narrowed as if he sensed vulnerability. "What, exactly, is your job?"

Max side-eyed him. "I own a club in Manhattan."

Nancy practically bounced in her seat. "Oooh, my boyfriend and I are visiting the big city in a couple months. You'll have to give us the address, so we can be sure to check it out when we're there."

So Max owned a club in the city. My interest was piqued. Perhaps Nancy wouldn't be the only one visiting him. Maybe I could too. Like a stalker. A pathetic sex-is-now-spoiled-with-all-other-men kind of stalker.

"Kate never mentioned you owned a club." Shawn appeared to think he'd sniffed out something worthy of criticism.

Max shrugged. "My club is exclusive to members, and my sister undoubtedly knew I wouldn't let someone like you through the doors."

Shawn's eyes flashed with anger, but he said nothing. Max had put him in his place yet again.

After dinner, they took a number of pictures of the bridal party. I witnessed the tension between Max and his father as they watched from opposite corners. It was clear from their strained smiles that both were a heartbeat away from boiling over.

Of course Shawn found any excuse to stand next to me in the photos. Once we were watching the bride and groom do couple photos from the side, he came up to taunt me. "Watched your video last night."

He easily could have. Once my ex had released our sex video to the Internet, there was no controlling it. But I'd be damned if I'd let Shawn think he had the upper hand.

"Yeah, did you learn anything? Like a man with a small dick really ought to get better with his hands, Shawn. You've got to be sure to slow the video down and take some notes." I turned to walk away, but he snatched my arm. What was with the grabbiness? Before I could tell him to get his paws off me, someone else beat me to it.

"Let go of her fucking arm before I break yours," came Max's growl. His voice was low, but the anger radiating off of him was breathtaking.

Shawn immediately released me, allowing Max's eyes to focus on the fingerprints reddening my skin.

Sensing this was about to escalate, I put my hand on Max's chest. "Let's go. Okay?"

He didn't respond.

"Max, please." There were enough eggshells for him to step on without my adding more.

Finally, he focused his beautiful blues on me, making me suck in a breath.

"What's going on here?" Kate stalked toward us, her gaze bouncing between me and her brother.

Max eased his expression before turning to her. "Nothing. I'm going up to my room. Can't wait to see you in your dress tomorrow."

She sighed. "Before you go, will you take some pictures with me? Me and Tim?"

I was relieved Kate was including him in some way. It couldn't be easy for her to keep her parents and brother separate from each other while still trying to ensure they all felt included in her special weekend.

His smile was tight, but he nodded. "Of course."

After a few pictures, none of which included his parents, Max seemed to relax. Next up were more photos with the bridal party. By the time we were done, I was stifling a yawn. No wonder, since I hadn't gotten a lot of sleep last night. Nor would I get a lot tonight. The thought had me anxious to get upstairs.

"What's up with you and my brother?" Kate asked after the last snap.

I wasn't sure I cared for her judgmental tone. "What do you mean?"

"I mean the way you guys came down in the elevator earlier, and he switched your seats at the table?"

"We caught the same elevator going down to the restaurant with four other people, and he switched seats with me because he knew sitting next to Shawn would be uncomfortable for me."

Her eyes narrowed. "I think you need to be nicer to Shawn."

"Believe me when I say I'm plenty nice." She was the bride, and as her maid of honor, I was intent she had a great weekend. But frankly, Shawn had grown more aggressive, and I wouldn't suck it up just to save her feelings. After the wedding, there'd be an uncomfortable conversation in which she'd hear everything about Shawn, including my discovery she'd confided my secret to him.

"I don't understand what happened. He's a catch."

She made it sound as though I couldn't do better. "Kate, let's not get into it this weekend. You have enough tension going on in your family. You don't need to add into the mix a couple who went out on three whole dates. Okay?"

She expelled a long breath. "Okay. Yeah. Sorry, my dad is being an asshole, and my mom was crying earlier because seeing Max has been tough on her. Maybe I shouldn't have invited my brother to the wedding."

My temper threatened, but I reeled it in. "It's been tough on Max too, but I'm sure it would've been harder if you hadn't wanted him here."

"Perhaps. Any chance you can help with the wedding favors tonight? I mean you weren't around for any of the other prep, so it would be nice if you pitched in."

Again, I had to bite my tongue. She acted as though I hadn't done a thing for her shower six weeks ago when I'd taken a bus here. As for her bachelorette party in New York City, I'd be paying off the credit cards I'd used to fund it for months. But the biggest bummer was I didn't get to escape to my room. "Of course. Happy to help."

By the time I was done tying little bows around boxes of mints and sticking on a pretty label with the couple's name on them, it was late, and I was beat.

Yet the moment I walked in the hotel room door and spotted Max, my libido woke right up. He was lying against the headboard, shirtless and in flannel pajama bottoms.

"Hi," I greeted, slipping off one shoe at a time.

He was nursing a glass of amber liquid. "Hi. How were the bridal duties?"

"Tomorrow when you see your little box of mints by your table placement, look very impressed by the craftmanship in the tied bow."

He chuckled, set his drink by the bed and crossed the

room toward me. Tipping my chin up, he rubbed his thumb along my cheek. "You look exhausted."

"My face isn't actively reflecting what the rest of my body is thinking."

Again with the dimpled grin. Dropping his lips to mine, he pressed a chaste kiss against them.

"More, please."

"You need your rest."

"I really don't. I have a confession."

His brow jumped up. "Oh, yeah? Do I need to build another pillow wall to hear it?"

"Nope. This one I'll tell you without the pillows. I've been thinking about you all day."

My words had the opposite effect on him I'd anticipated. Instead of smiling, he frowned. "Oakley, I'm not the type—"

"Stop what you're about to say. I've been thinking about sex. Nothing else. And it's because last night was kind of dark. I'm sure I'll get one look at your penis tonight in the light and think, 'Eh, must've built it up in my head. I'm over it.'"

He threw his head back with laughter. "My apologies. I won't insult your intelligence again by telling you not to get attached. Truth is, I've been thinking about you today too. You might be the only reason I've managed to salvage today and I'm not a hundred miles away by now."

Dang. I'd convinced myself I wanted this man for sex alone, and then he had to go and say something sweet. "Tonight couldn't have been easy on you. I'm sorry."

"It's fine, but I can tell Kate regrets having me here."

It was on the tip of my tongue to argue, but I wouldn't defend a lie. "I think she'd regret it more if you weren't."

His eyes were sad. "I'm glad she invited me even if I am

counting the minutes until I can leave. Now then, enough talk about my family."

"Agreed. Where were we?"

His hands skimmed down my arms, causing goose bumps. "We were at the part where you kiss me, and this time it doesn't have to stop."

Thump. Thump. Some men had lines. Max simply said what was on his mind. I tipped up on my toes to lay my hand along his smooth face. He was a beautiful man. And all mine for the next two nights.

Brushing his lips with mine, I started out slow. I loved the power of a kiss. A kiss could be sensual, carnal, or intimate. I could ebb and flow based on my emotions, and right now, I needed sensual. Sexy and slow, our tongues tangled. Max wasn't in a hurry to get me into bed, and the anticipation of it all was intoxicating.

"Tell me more about your dreams, the ones which have you touching yourself in your sleep," he whispered in my ear while kissing down the curve of my neck.

"There's not much to tell." I wasn't ready to share my secret.

He leaned back so his gaze locked on mine. "I'll never judge you. I promise."

"It's too personal."

He sighed against my lips. "Ask *me* something personal, then."

The obvious question was to ask about the falling out with his parents, but it was too raw a subject and didn't fit the mood. Instead, I took a different road. "What do *you* fantasize about?"

His eyes sparkled. "This."

My brow arched. "Define this."

"A woman who is both sexy and fun, and who smiles

when she sees me. Anticipating all day the thought of getting you alone. I know it sounds odd, but a normal weekend with a normal girl where we enjoy one another without any pressure or pretense is my fantasy."

Normal. I repeated the word in my head and let the disappointment sink into me. He wanted a normal girl. Normal girls didn't dream about getting fucked in front of other people.

"Your turn."

Yeah, not after his confession. So I did what I'd always done. I tamped down on my real feelings and went with what was comfortable. "I liked what we did last night." I wasn't lying. Last night had been hot, and tonight was bound to be off the charts. Telling him the truth about my fantasies would only make us both feel uncomfortable. It wasn't as if he could give me my fantasy this weekend anyway, so why bother telling him?

He cocked his head to the side as if studying me. "Are you sure?"

"Yes. I enjoyed being tied up. Liked when you talked dirty to me."

Was that disappointment flickering in his gaze? No, it couldn't be if he'd told me he wanted "normal."

He grabbed his whiskey and sat in the wingback chair. "Strip for me." Leaning back easily, he appeared to be waiting for the show.

I'd never undressed in front of a man the way he'd just requested. Usually when getting naked, there was the hurry of taking off one another's clothes. It wasn't slow and purposeful. But I was up for it. My dress came first, pooling at my feet.

The way Max tracked every movement with heat in his eyes was intoxicating. My fantasy had always concentrated on the idea of "other" people watching, but having him watch me like this hit buttons I didn't know would give me a rush. My bra and thong came off next.

"You're so fucking sexy. Come closer."

The air crackled with electricity as I took a few steps toward him.

"Stop."

I was inches away. When he leaned forward and inhaled my pussy, my knees nearly buckled. I tilted forward, ready for him to taste me, but he wouldn't be rushed. At least not yet.

His fingers eased inside of me. I'd normally be embarrassed with how wet I already was, but his growl disrupted any negative thoughts. His eyes turned molten; his hot gaze burned into my face.

"Brace yourself by holding on to my shoulders."

I needed to, especially when he shoved three fingers inside of me. His fingers were relentless in their delicious assault, and before I knew it, I was panting with need, my body shaking with such force I wasn't sure how much longer I could keep upright.

My fingernails dug into Max's shoulders as my climax washed over me.

He looked up, tasting his fingers as though he couldn't get enough. Jesus.

He stood up and made quick work of losing his pajama bottoms, showing he was commando underneath. When he put on a condom, I could see the light hadn't been playing tricks last night. He was as large as I remembered.

Putting his hands under my ass, he lifted me up.

"What are you doing?"

"Keeping the bed a no-sex bed. Wrap your legs around me."

He didn't have to ask me twice. The next moment, he walked across the room and put me against the wall. Lining himself up, he thrust home. There was a tinge of pain, but it faded once he held still, letting me accommodate to his size. I gasped when he pulled out and shoved back in. Now it was all pleasure.

"You like it when I fuck you against the wall?"

"Yes." I opened my eyes and spied the window on the other side of the room. Before I could overthink it, I voiced my want. "Move me to the window."

He stilled. "Yeah?"

"Yeah. It's snowing, and I want to feel the cold." He didn't need to know the real reason I wanted us against the window.

He lifted me off his cock to set me on my feet and led me over to the floor-to-ceiling window. "Here?"

"Yes." God, my adrenaline started to spike. It careened into overdrive when he spun me around and placed my hands on the glass. Once he was behind me, his fingers slipped between my legs.

But then he was suddenly gone.

"Hold on." Stepping in front of me, he pressed on the glass.

"What are you doing?"

He glanced over with a sheepish expression. "Ensuring you don't fall out. It wouldn't be a good look for the brother of the bride to fuck the maid of honor out the fourth-story window of the hotel the night before the wedding."

I was overtaken by a fit of giggles. "It would be quite the shame."

He grinned and returned my hands to the window in front of me. "It really would. Now, where were we?"

His fingers found me wet and more than ready. “Lean forward, ass in the air.”

I moaned once he pushed inside of me again.

“What do you see?” His breath was hot on the back of my neck.

“Snow.” It was falling at a rapid pace now, beautiful and peaceful. A frozen contrast to the heat between us.

“What else? Do you see cars parked outside? Maybe someone is looking up at us right now. Do you think they can see your incredible body silhouetted in the window and know you’re getting fucked against it?”

The oxygen in the room evaporated, and he pumped into me with vigor. My orgasm tore through me with a force I hadn’t expected. My face dropped against the glass, my knees threatened to give out. But he held me tight with his arm banded around my waist, emptying himself inside of me with a roar of satisfaction.

Chapter Fourteen

MAX

I wasn't often surprised when it came to sex, but Oakley's request to fuck her in the window had done the job. I'd thought the exercise would be a delightful deviation from my plans to keep things rather tame, but watching the magnitude of her climax was my undoing. Fuck, with the way her pussy was milking me, I couldn't hold back any longer.

Sliding out slowly, I enjoyed the way she mewled at the loss of contact. I turned her around in my arms, supporting her upright and smiling at the dazed expression on her face.

"Kiss me," she whispered.

I could do it for days. Her kisses were a combination of sexy and sweet. I'd never craved this type of intimacy before.

But it was evident she was exhausted. The long day had depleted her, both mentally and physically. After lifting her up, I carried her to the bed. I attempted to put her down, but she clung to me like a koala.

Chuckling, I settled her in the bed and kissed her forehead. "I'll return in a moment."

After disposing of the condom, and brushing my teeth, I climbed into bed with her, pulling her close.

"What time do you need to be up?"

"Seven. I already set my alarm. We have hair and makeup and are hanging with the bride all morning," she muttered into my chest.

Selfishly, I wished we had all day to stay in bed. Oh, the plans I could make for her which would include exploring her unexpected turn-on at having sex in the window. Perhaps there was a kinky side to her she'd yet to discover.

"I wish we could stay in bed all day drinking beer and eating chicken nachos with a big side of guacamole."

My chest rumbled with laughter. "You have an oddly specific food-driven fantasy."

"It's to sustain us while we have a ton of sex. Imagine all of the surfaces we've yet to try."

"We'd save the bed for last, of course."

"Of course. It's not called the no-sex bed for nothing," she whispered, followed by a yawn.

"Get some sleep, beautiful."

"'Kay."

I lay awake for a good hour, listening to the soft breaths of the woman entwined with me. A startling vision creeped into my mind. What would it be like to come home to someone each night and hold her like this?

I barely knew Oakley, and yet there was a familiarity and comfort between us. Perhaps it came from growing up in the same town and knowing one another when we were younger, or maybe it was the way we clicked when it came to our humor and personalities. All I knew was I wanted more, and I had to remind myself why it wasn't possible. I'd be asking her to give up too much of her future.

The next morning came early, and while I was used to

operating on little sleep, I doubted Oakley was. So after my run, I grabbed coffee and a couple of breakfast sandwiches before returning to the room.

She was a vision, sprawled out on the bed on her back, naked and gorgeous. Glancing at the clock, I saw we had limited time before she had to get ready. With that in mind, I put down the coffee and food, deciding there was only one way to wake her.

"Oh, God, Max," she moaned the moment my mouth touched her center.

I loved the way she said my name. "Good morning."

Her hooded eyes looked down and locked with mine. "The best morning I can think of."

Within minutes, I had her squirming beneath me, panting and coming in my mouth. It was tempting to go for another orgasm, but her phone alarm filled the room.

"Any chance your sister could delay the wedding? Just an hour or two would be nice."

I chuckled, getting up to grab her coffee. "I'm afraid not, but I brought you coffee. Not sure how you like it, so I brought cream and sugar."

She smiled like I'd given her the very best gift. "My hero. I prefer it black like my soul." She sipped, smiling after her first taste.

There was nothing black about her soul. Instead, I ventured to guess it was new and pristine. Mine on the other hand... Well, according to my father, it was most definitely dark.

"I got you some breakfast too. I'm gonna run your shower and get the water warm."

Suddenly I was overwhelmed with emotion. Here I was worried about her getting attached, but the opposite seemed to be happening. I was torturing myself with a glimpse of something I couldn't have.

"Hey, what's wrong?" came her voice behind me.

I forced a smile. "Nothing. Water's ready."

"You should join me."

"If I join you, you'll be late."

Her lips curved up in a smile. "I think I can be a little bit late."

Chapter Fifteen

OAKLEY

I was five minutes late when I knocked on Kate's hotel room door. She had a large suite on the other side of the hotel to be used solely by us women today.

"About time," she huffed when Nancy let me in through the door. She was seated in a chair, having her long hair detangled by the stylist.

"Sorry." I wasn't at all sorry. Being fucked against the shower wall by Max was worth the five minutes' tardiness. And let's face it, five minutes wasn't exactly criminal.

"Yeah, well, I needed you here on time, and when you weren't, I had to send Lara for coffee."

Oh, boy. Bridezilla was in full effect. "Like I said, sorry. What can I do for you now?"

Kate seemed to calm down some. "I'd like it if you could go down to Tim's suite and give him my rings."

"Of course, happy to do it." Anything to get out of the tension-filled room.

Unfortunately my relief didn't last once Shawn answered the door of Tim's room. "Hi, whore," he greeted with a sneer.

Tim, who was standing right behind him, frowned at his friend. "What the hell, man?"

Shawn turned red, obviously not liking a witness to his abhorrent behavior. Turning on his heel, he left us at the door.

"You might want to rethink being friends with this one, Tim. Kate sent me down here to give you her rings. Here you go." I handed over the velvet box.

"Sorry, Oakley. I had no idea things were so bad between you two."

"Yeah, well, do me a favor and don't tell Kate." She'd probably find a way to blame me. "I don't want any wedding drama." I'd always liked Tim. Whereas Kate could sometimes be high-strung, he'd always been laid-back and chill. Best of all, he treated her like a queen and genuinely loved her.

He gave me a soft smile. "Agreed. Thanks."

By noon, I was ready to pull my hair out from all of the errands and "bridal festivities." But Kate was in her element, surrounded by friends and family who were catering to her every whim. My hair had been twisted into an elaborate, bride-approved updo, and my makeup tastefully applied. What I wouldn't have given for a big, greasy snack about now. None of the lousy finger sandwiches sitting on the platter for people to pick at.

"Hey, Oakley," Kate said, looking at her phone.

"Yeah?"

"My brother has something for me. He asked if you could go by his room and pick it up. He's in room four twenty-seven."

I tried not to look giddy at the prospect. "Sure. Happy to. Be right back."

"Make it quick because we're putting on our dresses in

fifteen minutes. Right after that, we're heading downstairs to start pictures."

"Will do."

I couldn't wait for this day to be over. If I ever decided to get married, which I wasn't sure I wanted, I'd opt for a small elopement. No monogrammed robes, women's brunches, or hair-and-makeup parties.

I'd barely opened the hotel room door when Max pulled me inside. He wasted no time capturing my lips in a kiss.

"Hi," he murmured in my ear.

"Hi." Dammit, I couldn't afford to be late again. "I only have thirteen minutes and forty-seven seconds remaining before you sister has a complete conniption over me being late again."

He grinned against my lips. "Better eat fast."

"What?" I looked beyond him to see a huge pile of chicken nachos, a side of guacamole, and two beers on the small table set for two.

"I might not be able to offer up the naked time together, but I figured two out of the three things might be a nice surprise."

It was beyond thoughtful. "It's a good thing for you the sex is so great between us; otherwise, I might say this is the highlight of my day."

He chuckled. "Good thing. Come on."

The beer tasted divine, the nachos even better. We both grinned the entire time while I tried not to make a total pig of myself during the next few minutes. "My Spanx will not thank me for this, but my stomach sure does. Thank you."

"You're welcome. Oh, and before I forget, here's the gift for Kate."

"What is it?" I asked, taking the long wrapped box.

"It's a bracelet with her birthstone. Anyhow, better chug-a-lug. You've got four minutes."

I finished my beer, brushed my teeth, and shared one last kiss with him at the door. Then I was off to the bridal suite with a big goofy grin on my face. Two minutes to spare.

"Where have you been?" Kate asked the moment I stepped inside. All eyes swung to me, and I saw immediately I was the only one not already in her dress. So much for having fifteen minutes.

"I had to go back to my room and use the restroom before getting your gift from Max."

She perked up when I held out the box. "Okay, fine, get dressed."

Ugh. When was this day going to be over again? I quickly changed into the red dress, thankful Kate had made them simple instead of fussy. The strapless bust was flattering, as was the A-line skirt. As I walked out of the dressing area, I could see Kate holding up a beautiful diamond-and-sapphire bracelet from the box Max had given her.

"It's stunning," I said amongst the murmurs of everyone else saying something similar.

"He said it's my something new and blue in case I didn't have anything. It's so sweet."

Thank God she put it on. Max might not ever admit it, but I knew it would hurt him deeply if she refused his gift.

In the church, the ceremony was lovely. As much as I tried to pay attention to the vows, my gaze kept wandering toward Max, sitting in the back with Fran and Dan. It had been years since I'd seen them, and I was pleased they had each other to talk to.

The reception was held at the hotel in the large ballroom. By the time I was done with the bridal-party pictures, I'd completely had it with Shawn. He'd started drinking and was getting meaner by the minute. It didn't help that Kate put the entire wedding party at the head table, and I had no choice this time but to take my seat next to him.

"You ready for our dance?" Shawn slurred, the strong smell of tequila on his breath.

There would be a bridal-party dance, and I could not have dreaded it more. I consoled myself with the notion that after tomorrow morning's brunch, I'd never have to see him again. Which begged the question: how was I getting home? Max and I hadn't talked about it, but since he lived in New York City, I hoped he could drop me off on his way home. I wondered if he'd chosen to skip the reception since I hadn't seen him since leaving the church.

I cringed when the DJ announced the first dance of the bride and groom. Which meant my dance with Shawn was coming up soon. Getting out of my seat, I walked with the other two bridesmaids toward the dance floor. Was there any way I could ditch Shawn without making a scene? He looked way too eager to take my hand. Once again, I found myself searching for Max.

"You're pathetic," Shawn hissed, sliding his hand down to my ass.

I lifted his hand up. "Right. I'm the pathetic one."

"If you ask nicely, I'll give you a ride back to the city tomorrow."

"My quota for dealing with psychopath drivers has been filled this month, so I'll pass."

"A man like Max would never be into a whore like you."

"Ah, there's the psychopath I've gotten to know so well."

This song could not be over soon enough. I finally found Max. He was standing near the bar, his gaze fixed on us. I wasn't the only one to spot him. Shawn pulled me closer in a show of possession. Max's eyes narrowed.

My dance partner wasn't done. As soon as the song stopped, he smashed his lips to mine. What the hell? I pushed on his chest. "Let go of me."

He laughed. "Wouldn't want to make a scene."

I wanted nothing more than to slap his face. "You know what the best thing about this dance was?"

"What?"

"It's the last time I'll ever have to touch you."

Max's voice was suddenly beside me. "May I have this dance?" Although he was smiling, the set of his jaw left no doubt he was angry.

"Of course you can," I said, immensely relieved to take his hand.

"Great. Let's go." He whisked me off before Shawn could utter a word.

"Incredible sex, chicken nachos, beer—and another save from Shawn the psycho. It's like you really are my superhero."

His features softened. "I wanted to punch his face, especially when he kissed you."

"Jealous?" I said it jokingly, but he was dead serious with his answer.

"Yes, very."

Wait. What? He was?

"I hated seeing you on his arm at the wedding, loathed watching you seated next to each other during dinner, and as previously discussed, wanted to punch his face for kissing you."

"You and me both. Your sister loved the bracelet, by the way."

He relaxed. "I'm glad. I think a small part of me feared she might not want to wear it because of my parents. Stupid, right?"

"No. It's not stupid at all." I wished I could comfort him with a caress or a kiss. But I couldn't, not out here on the dance floor.

After the dance ended, he led me over to a table toward the back. "Come on, I have some people I want to introduce you to."

Chapter Sixteen

MAX

It was tough being ignored by my parents at the church and watching others notice me there and whisper. And then there was watching from the sidelines as photos were taken of the happy couple with their loved ones outside the church. I hadn't been asked to step in for any family photos. Not like they wanted one with me in it to hang above the mantel and be reminded of my presence. It hurt. As much as I told myself it didn't, there was no way around it.

Now I was hanging around at the reception for one reason only. Oakley.

Jealousy wasn't often an emotion I entertained, but watching Shawn with his hands on her had made me want to stomp out to the dance floor and tear her away. Although I'd promised myself to keep my distance from her this evening for fear my parents might judge her poorly as a result, I couldn't help asking her to dance, at least once. I'd use any excuse to touch her in public while I counted the minutes until I could get her alone.

After the dance, however, I wasn't yet ready to part

company. And chose instead to introduce her to Fran and Dan.

I was surprised when Fran jumped up to hug her. "Oakley, you look absolutely beautiful."

"Thank you, Fran. You haven't aged a bit, and, Dan, looking handsome in your suit."

The older man blushed and also gave her a hug.

"I didn't realize you all knew each other," I commented.

Fran tsked. "Oakley used to waitress for us during the summers when she was in high school."

Small world. "Did you really?"

She smiled. "I sure did. Best breakfast burrito in town. Wish I'd had time to get over there this weekend."

"You were busy, and we understand. It sure is nice to see you. Matter of fact, watching you two dancing together made my old heart happy. Anyhow, although it's great to see you both, we're bidding good night to the bride and groom and then skedaddling home. Early morning at the diner and all."

We all said our goodbyes and watched them walk off to find Kate and Tim.

"They haven't changed a bit," Oakley murmured with a smile.

"I know, right? They're good people."

"The best. So without this sounding weird, going my way tomorrow morning?"

I'd assumed I'd be giving her a ride home. "Of course. I'd be happy to drive you home. Thought we'd leave first thing in the morning."

"Oh, well, there's the breakfast thing at nine."

"We can wait until after." I hadn't been invited to the breakfast, but it was just as well. I'd be happier staying up in the room and avoiding my family.

She took my hand. "You're coming, right?"

"Nah. I'm about tapped out regarding family time. But I'm happy to wait for you. We'll leave after."

"What are you two doing?" came my sister's voice. She'd walked up and was staring where Oakley had taken my hand.

"I was telling Oakley I wanted to ask you to dance, and she was assuring me you'd say yes."

Kate flashed a brilliant smile. "As if I wouldn't say yes, big brother. Come on."

I could feel everyone's eyes on us the moment we stepped out to the floor. Especially my father's. Anger simmered in his gaze.

Good, because I had plenty simmering in me too. He might not agree with my choices. He might not want me as part of his family, but he sure as hell didn't get to make that decision for Kate. "You look beautiful. And happy."

"Thank you. I loved the bracelet, by the way."

"Glad you did."

"I haven't had a chance to talk to you a lot this weekend. Sorry I've been so busy."

"Don't be. It's your wedding. I'm glad I could be here for it. Where's the honeymoon?"

"The Bahamas. Tim surprised me with it. I've never been anywhere tropical, so it should be fun. We're hoping for a honeymoon baby, so how better to spend it?"

I nearly missed a step. "Wow, you're moving fast."

"I want to be a mom more than anything. Just like all my friends; it's all we talk about."

"Yeah. Does Oakley have the same plans?" I knew better than to ask, but I did it anyhow hoping she'd say —what? No?

"Of course she does. I'm convinced the city thing is only until she finds the right guy she can settle down with. Then I think she'll move home. We even picked out our future kids' names. I chose Savannah if it was a girl, and she chose Madison."

Fuck, I should've known better than to ask. I swallowed hard at the confirmation of what I already knew. "You'll make a terrific mother."

"Thanks." She went on to describe the house Tim had bought and how she'd decorate it. I smiled and nodded in all the right places, but the reality was we lived in two different worlds. And so did Oakley and I.

After the dance, I should've gone up to my room. It was a win for the night to have seen my little sister married, shared a dance, and not fought with my family. But knowing Oakley was here until the end meant I didn't want to leave her. Not with Shawn getting drunker by the minute.

As things wound down, and people started to leave, I found her taking out gifts from the rear of the ballroom.

"Here, I'll help," I offered, assisting her in filling up a rolling cart. We pulled it out the back door where Tim's SUV was parked.

It was frigid outside, which had her shivering in her dress.

"Here, take this." I took off my suit jacket and wrapped it around her shoulders, rubbing them to get her warm. And because we were alone, I dipped my head to her ear. "I can't wait to get you upstairs and properly warmed up." I had plans to explore what we'd started last night. Plans to discover what other things turned Oakley on. If we only had one night remaining, I intended to make the most of it.

"Well, well, isn't this cute? Guess one man's trash really can become another man's trash," came the slurred words.

I looked over to see Shawn carrying a few things out along with another groomsman.

"More like treasure, but you're both drunk and stupid, so I understand how you got it mixed up."

The other groomsman chuckled along with Oakley, which in turn irritated Shawn. Good. The asshole should be taken down a notch.

Oakley scooted by him to grab the centerpiece from the other groomsman. “Thanks, Andy, I’ll put this in the backseat so it doesn’t get crushed.”

But as she moved to take it, Shawn grabbed her arm, “I’ll put it in the seat, you stupid—”

He didn’t have a chance to finish before I had him up against the brick wall, my hand around his throat. I wasn’t a violent man, but watching him think he could put his hands on her and speak to her that way was my final straw.

“You don’t touch her. You don’t look at her. And you never speak to her again, do you understand?” Forget threatening to call his boss—I wanted to end him.

His reddened face let me know there was enough pressure he couldn’t get in a full breath.

“Nod if you understand, asshole.”

He nodded, and after one last press, just a reminder he was at my mercy, I let him go.

He crumpled to the ground, coughing and wheezing to get air.

“What the hell is going on here?”

Turning, I saw my father standing there beside my mother who had a centerpiece in her arms.

I swallowed hard, trying to calm down. “Shawn here needed a lesson on how to treat women.”

My dad barked out a bitter laugh. “That’s rich coming from you, don’t you think?”

“Meaning what, exactly?” My fist clenched. The man hadn’t spared any words for me in a decade, and this was where he wanted to make his stand? Fine. I was more than ready for a fight.

"Meaning the way you treat women is reprehensible."

I nearly balked at his raw contempt. How had this been the man who'd coached me in Little League and taught me how to change a tire? How could he hate me the way he did?

"Phil, please," came my mother's shaky voice.

Shit. Seeing tears gathering in her eyes deflated me. All my fight was replaced with resignation. Why bother? I didn't want my dad's approval, and it was clear I no longer had my mother's love. "It's okay, Mom. I'm leaving." I turned toward Oakley. "Ready?"

My father stepped to block our path. "I won't let you corrupt this young lady the way you have the others at your deviant club. She can stay here with us."

Oakley's eyes went big at his words.

But for the first time, I refused to feel shame. Not after all these years of beating myself up for my choices. Something occurred to me. Unless they were my father's choices, I'd never please him.

My voice was calm. "My club is not deviant; it's sex, Dad. People have it. Matter of fact, I seem to remember you being all about telling me to have it in high school and college. Sow my wild oats, I believe you called it. But all of a sudden you act as though I'm the disgrace. You know what? You are. You're a hypocrite. I created a successful business, one you might not approve of, but one I'm proud of owning."

His entire face turned red. "You're going to hell."

A humorless chuckle left my throat. "For what? Defying you and dropping out of law school? Owning a successful club which allows people to be safe and explore their sexuality without judgment? For being a loving brother and son who never deserved to be cut off just because you didn't agree with my choices?" I turned toward my mom. "I know this isn't what you wanted for me, but I'm still the boy you loved. I'm sorry I disappointed you, Mom, but you disappointed me too. You were supposed to love me unconditionally."

Tears streamed down her face while I held mine back. Barely. At the crux of it all, losing her love was the one thing I doubted I'd ever get over.

My father didn't answer. He was an angry little man who threw out his judgments without anything to back them up except it just wasn't his way. And my mom had simply never been strong enough to go against him. I found myself feeling sorry for her instead of angry.

"Come on, Oakley."

Much to my relief, she took my hand, but my father turned to her.

"If you go with him, I'll call up your parents right now, young lady, and tell them—"

If I'd expected Oakley to pale with the threat, I was mistaken. Instead, her eyes flashed with anger.

"Tell them what? That your son has treated me with nothing but respect? Unlike others who left me stranded on the side of the road because they had a fit of road rage like a psychopath. You want to start lecturing young men about their abhorrent behavior, start with that misogynist asshole." She pointed toward Shawn. "And if you want to call my parents, be my guest. Unlike you, they would never cut off their child because they don't agree with my choices."

Chapter Seventeen

OAKLEY

I had the pleasure of watching Max's father's face go red. Just when he was about to respond with something I was sure would be uttered in a yell, Max's mother stepped up. "That's enough, Phil."

She gave me a nod as if to say, "go."

I was more than ready to leave. As I pulled Max away and down the hall, I was pretty sure I could hear her giving his father an earful. Good. I was still radiating anger on his behalf. How could his father be so hateful?

It was enough to almost distract me from the bombshell about Max owning a sex club.

As soon as we were in the lobby, Max pulled me into the alcove for the wine tasting room, framing my face with his hands.

"I've never had someone defend me the way you just did." His lips took mine in a searing kiss.

Damn, I melted into him.

"What the hell are you doing?"

We broke apart to see none other than the bride standing at the entrance. Next to her was the groom.

Kate's face went into a rage, one she directly focused on me. "I can't believe this. I trusted you."

Was I in the twilight zone? I was making out with her very single brother, not her husband.

Max tried to divert. "Kate, calm down."

She flicked her gaze to him briefly before verbally assaulting me. "Is this why you've been so rude to Shawn? It's like I don't even know you anymore. You think you're too good for this town, too good for me."

Tim spoke up, grabbing her hand. "Babe, not here, not now."

But Kate wasn't listening to her new husband. "No, I think this is the perfect time. You've been the worst friend since you left for college, and you've been distracted this entire weekend. And now I know why. You've been sleeping with my brother."

"Kate, that's enough," interjected Max, but I put my hand on his chest. I was trying not to say something I would later regret.

"Maybe your ex-boyfriend, Evan, was right about you."

I sucked in a breath while both Tim and Max shared a baffled look. But I knew what she meant. She was calling me a slut. Shaming me about what I'd thought had been an intimate moment between two people had become public. My so-called best friend went there.

"You know what, Kate, I think it's clear our friendship has run its course. You want to think it's because I'm a bad friend, you go on and believe that. I'm done." I brushed by her and left before I could say more.

My tears were hot and angry as I strode toward the elevator. I swiped at them, frustrated by their existence. There had been an edge to Kate for months, and especially this weekend, but never could I have imagined she'd attack me the way she had.

Max was on my heels. In the elevator, he took my hand but didn't say a word. Once we were in the hotel room, he dragged out my suitcase and his bag and placed them both on the bed.

"We're leaving."

All my adrenaline had left the building. In its place was sheer exhaustion mixed with sadness. For a moment I considered the breakfast tomorrow but then realized I no longer had a best friend who wanted me there. Yeah, leaving sounded like the best option.

While I finished putting everything in my suitcase, Max called down to the front desk.

"We're all checked out."

I nodded, unable to find my voice.

He strode over, cupping my chin with his hand and kissing me swiftly. "Come on, let's go."

It wasn't until I was in his vehicle that I realized I was still wearing my bridesmaid gown. "I should've changed," I whispered in the dark as Max turned onto the main road.

"I'm sorry I rushed you. I can pull over and bring your clothes up here."

"No, no, it's fine."

He glanced over. "Oakley, this is all my fault. I'm so sorry."

I faced him in the darkened cab. "How is any of this your fault?"

"Me being here this weekend was the catalyst for everything."

"No, it wasn't. Shawn dumped me on the side of the highway. You had nothing to do with his road rage or how he treated me. Kate has been angry with me since I decided to stay in New York City and live a different life from her. And she told Shawn about my video. You had nothing to do with any of that, either."

"I can't believe Kate said those things to you."

In some way, deep down, I wasn't surprised. We'd been growing apart for a while. "She never forgave me for staying away after college. It's like she saw my not wanting to move home as a rejection of her and our friendship. We want different futures, and she's angry about it. This was the last straw."

He turned to stare at me. "Different futures how?"

"Different in every way."

He appeared to want to ask more questions, but I had a few of my own. "You own a sex club?"

He winced. "I should've told you."

"Can you tell me now? How did it come about?"

He sighed. "Eleven years ago, my best friend Shane and I met a woman in New York City. She had a club. It was smaller back then, and Shane and I became regulars. Then when she wanted to sell, Shane and I bought it. We remodeled and recreated it to be more upscale. We've been operating it ever since the grand reopening."

"How did your parents find out?" Owning a sex club didn't seem like the thing you'd bring up over Thanksgiving dinner.

Another sigh. "I dropped out of law school and went home to tell them. After getting the lecture about throwing my life away, I told them I was investing in a club. I didn't say what kind, but it didn't matter. There was no pleasing my father once I quit law school. I underestimated his sleuthing skills, though. He found out what Club Travesty really was, and well, then he had all the ammunition he needed to call me a disgrace and tell me I would no longer be part of the family if I continued on that path."

"He issued an ultimatum."

"Yeah, and I'm finally coming to realize that unless the result is me crawling back to him for a big 'I told you so,' he'll never be happy. Sex club, nightclub, curing cancer—my dad's love was always conditional on the premise I follow in his footsteps and become just like him."

"He was way out of line tonight. Whether he agreed with your choices or not, he had no right to speak to you the way he did. I was glad to see your mother'd had enough too."

His brow furrowed. "What do you mean?"

"I mean when she told him to stop. She was arguing with him when we left. Did you not notice?"

"Guess I didn't pay attention to it. Are you angry I didn't tell you about owning the club?"

"Why would I be? Your secret is something you choose to share or not."

"I almost told you the first night. I just didn't want to ruin it."

My nose scrunched up in confusion. "Did you think if I'd known about the club, I wouldn't have wanted to sleep with you?" Quite the opposite.

"Yeah. But I don't only own the club; I also perform there. It felt good for a change to have a normal weekend with a sexy woman without it being about the club."

There was that word again. Normal. "Can I ask you something?"

"Anything."

"When you perform, is there adrenaline from knowing you're being watched?" Picturing it made my body tingle.

"At first, yes, but I guess the novelty wears off after a while. I got burnt out."

Not the answer I wanted to hear. "I see."

He sighed. "It's tough to explain, but at the club you and your partner are performing for everyone else's pleasure. Not your own."

"You're putting on an act?"

"Yes. I'm not saying it's not enjoyable, but when it's your job, you lose some of your enthusiasm for it. I don't mean to burst your bubble about what it's like."

Dammit. He had. A little. I'd assumed his performances were as hot for him as they were for the spectators. "Who, um, are the women you're with?"

It was the first time I'd seen him truly uncomfortable, and I wondered if his dad's comments were in the back of his mind. "Some of the women from the club. They're performers too. It's all consensual."

Of course it would be. Given Max's skill as a lover, I would bet there were any number of women lined up to perform with him.

He cleared his voice. "We shouldn't be talking about this."

"Why not?" I had a lot more questions.

"Because the club isn't your world."

"That's your father's voice in your head. You said the club is a place where people can go and not feel judged. Did you mean it?"

"Of course I did."

"Then I'm ready to tell you my fantasy. The truth this time."

He took the next exit and pulled off onto the side of the road.

MAX

I turned toward her in the darkened cab of my SUV. "Tell me."

"I have a fantasy about being watched." She covered her face with her hands as if she couldn't believe the words had come out of her mouth.

"Watched how? Like the window last night where you could think someone might see you?"

"Yes, but more. Like being on display."

"Details, Oakley. I need details." I craved them desperately.

"I want to be blindfolded and completely in the dark about who is watching. It could be one person or a dozen. It could be hundreds of people crowded around. And I don't know which of those is true. I want someone who will talk me through it and for me to trust him enough to know I'm safe."

I adjusted my trousers as I was quickly getting hard. "Trust is the most important part. Did you attempt this fantasy with your ex?"

"I told him I liked the idea of us watching it later, and that's how the stupid video came to be. Guess you could say I was experimenting with my fantasy. But then, of course, he called me a slut and put it on the Internet. And I told my best friend about my humiliation, and now it turns out she also thinks I'm a slut."

I was angry on her behalf. No one should be shamed for their sexual preference or fantasies. Ever. Yet hadn't I made an art out of shaming myself? Oakley was right. My father's voice was in my head. And I'd allowed it to stay there rent-free for too long. I was done. It was time I started believing the words I preached to others.

"You're not a slut. And your fantasy about wanting to be watched isn't anything to be ashamed of. Your ex was a fool. Any man would be lucky to fulfill your fantasies for you."

And suddenly I wanted to be that man.

Chapter Eighteen

OAKLEY

I wanted Max to take me to his club more than anything, but I wasn't sure how to ask. Especially given he'd told me he was burnt out from performing. So instead I typed my address into the SUV's GPS to guide us to my apartment.

My eyes felt heavy as we got onto the highway, and I took the opportunity to sleep once Max got up to speed. I woke to the sound of the map lady on the GPS telling Max to take the next exit toward Jersey City and my apartment. Glancing over, I could see him concentrated on the road, his jaw set, tie undone, looking so very handsome.

"Sorry I fell asleep."

"Don't be. You needed the rest."

"This is me coming up."

He didn't deviate or exit. Didn't acknowledge my words. Didn't pay attention to the voice from my phone which now said, "Recalculating."

"Um, Max. You missed my exit."

Finally, he glanced over. "I know."

Okay. "Where are we going?"

"The club. Time to live out your fantasy."

Words I never thought I'd hear. So many emotions coursed through me at the same time. Nerves, anxiety, excitement. Was this truly happening?

We arrived in Manhattan after one in the morning. Max used a card to swipe into a garage, and parked his car on the third level.

He took my hand, wordlessly leading me into a keycard-activated elevator. From there, we went down to the street level, through the back door of a nondescript building, down a corridor, and then Max swiped his card again to lead me into a small room. It looked to be an interview room of some sort.

"If you've changed your mind—"

"I haven't." Yes, I was nervous, but I needed this. Needed to fulfill the fantasy which had consumed my nights.

"We should discuss boundaries, and what you want to happen."

"I've told you my fantasy. Beyond that, I want you to decide what happens. I trust you, Max."

His eyes blazed with arousal. "Come with me."

He led me out of the room and down the hallway to yet another door requiring a swipe. On the other side of it a large man stood, dressed in an all-black suit.

"Good evening, Chuck. Are there any open viewing rooms?"

The larger man fastened his gaze on me before turning it back toward Max. "Good evening, boss. Let me check for you." He spoke into a discreet Bluetooth device fastened to his tie and nodded when something must've come through on his earpiece. "Yes, sir, room number four is available."

"Thank you."

I didn't miss the way the man looked at me curiously. Nor

the inquisitive gazes of a few of the other people we passed on the way to room number four. Must have been the red bridesmaid dress.

Once Max opened the door of number four, I was able to see how opulent the room was, from the dark wooden floors to the beautiful four-poster bed in the center. I noted the large velvet curtains covering what appeared to be viewing windows. I swallowed hard. "How will it work?"

"I'll open the curtains to one or more of the viewing rooms once we're ready. Could be a couple, could be a crowd, but you won't know. Unless you've changed your mind?"

"I haven't." He was giving me exactly what I'd asked for, and I was shaking in anticipation.

But when I studied Max, I realized he was nervous. I reached out to lay a hand along his cheek. "Did you change your mind?"

His lips tipped up in his trademark boyish grin. "No, but I've never done anything in these rooms when it wasn't a choreographed event. It's like two worlds have collided."

I thought I understood. Especially since he'd spoken of being burned out on performance. "How about we start with you kissing me and go from there?"

He took my lips. Damn. The man could kiss. Like the beat of a song, he varied his rhythm and tempo, tasting a little with his tongue, then going deeper, then sweeter. My head was already spinning and the clothes hadn't even come off. My hands remembered they could be part of the action and skimmed up each of his biceps where I could feel the solid muscles beneath his dress shirt. As I explored up to his shoulders and down to his chest, I became anxious to feel the heat of his skin on mine. Diving under the material, I enjoyed the way his muscles jumped at the contact of my palm against his hard chest.

As if reading my mind, he stepped back, unbuttoning his shirt to take it off and throw it on the floor. Although I'd seen him naked before, something about being in this room heightened my senses. Max was exquisite. A specimen of the finest quality. I didn't know what to do first. Stare, lick, taste, touch him with my hands? "You're—I mean you're—just wow."

His grin wasn't cocky; in fact, it was rather shy from my unfiltered compliment.

Running my fingertips down his chest, I enjoyed the way he swallowed hard at the contact. We both seemed to be on the same page about not rushing this. About taking the time to explore one another. We'd been together before, but this time was different.

Deciding to raise my exploration to another level, I leaned forward to trail my fingers with my mouth. The sound of his sharp inhalation of breath was like a drug to me. It was intoxicating to know I could have an effect on this man. Once I tracked to his nipple, I gently pulled it between my teeth. I loved how his hand tangled in my hair. He pulled, forcing me to tip my face up for him.

He crashed his lips to mine, no longer patient and exploring, but instead demanding. I loved it. This. This was what I'd been missing in former lovers. The ability for them to be thoughtful and playful while also capable of taking charge and dominating. For me to feel free in being myself and admitting I loved both sides equally.

His hands attacked my dress, but it was soon apparent my dress wasn't giving up easily. "How the hell do I get you out of this thing?"

My giggle caused him to grin. "There's a hook at the top, then the zipper."

"Stupid, cockblocking hook."

"Wait until you get to the Spanx." I had the answer to why the undressing was never part of my fantasy. After a couple attempts on his part to get off my clothes, I took over. While I stripped down, he did the same. Once we were both naked, he wasted no time in lifting me up and setting me on the bed.

This bed was different than any other I'd encountered. It was covered with a red silk sheet, adorned with different-sized pillows, and boasted adjustable ties on each of the four posts. No need for a frilly comforter or blankets here.

Beside the bed was a nightstand, not unlike the type in my bedroom. Max opened the drawer and pulled out a satin blindfold. "Are you ready?"

I nodded, and as soon as he placed the blindfold over my eyes, the world went dark. He scooted me onto the mattress, gently grabbing my right wrist to place it in a restraint. Next was my left wrist. The cuffs were tight but padded and soft against my skin.

Being robbed of sight and restrained to the bed magnified my other senses. He hadn't touched me yet, but the sound of him walking around the room had me on edge with anticipation. When his soft footsteps came closer, I found myself tensing, but I turned toward him when I felt the weight of him getting on the bed.

"You're beautiful, Oakley, so fucking stunning. I could worship you for days."

I'd never felt more beautiful. I felt confident, and best of all, unashamed about sharing my ultimate fantasy with this man. I didn't have to wait any longer for it to come true.

"There's not a man watching right now who doesn't wish it was him in here about to taste you. Women too, for that matter."

My arousal dialed up a hundred notches. Now aware we were being watched, my body started to tremble.

"Fuck, you're wet thinking about the people staring at you, aren't you?"

I whimpered and felt his stubble on the inside of my thighs. It was like my dream, only this time instead of imagining it, I was living it. He peeled me open, licking through my slit before sucking my clit between his lips.

Never had I experienced a man more considerate of my enjoyment than his own. It was clear Max was in no hurry to seek his own pleasure from the way he inhaled my scent to the way he didn't leave one inch untouched as he savored my taste.

My breath staggered, and my hips threatened to lift off the bed. His hands gripped my thighs to hold me still while his mouth didn't relent in the delicious torture.

"I swear I'll never get enough of your sweet cunt," he murmured against me.

His crass words were unlike any I'd ever heard, and yet coming from him, they were a complete turn-on. My entire body tensed, waiting, anticipating, begging for more.

For a moment, I regretted the fact my hands were tied. I would've loved to have run my fingers through his hair and pulled him closer. Then suddenly he was all in, with a combo of lips, teeth, and tongue, bringing me to the brink before just as suddenly stopping. I huffed in disappointment. He'd never teased me like this before.

"Relax, beautiful, we have all night."

God, I was both excited and tortured by his statement. His smile ghosted against me as if he was enjoying my sweet torment. He spread my legs further apart and wedged a pillow under my lower back. I was now completely open to him. Displayed for him and all who were watching. The thought caused a shudder through my body. Was it possible to go mad with lust? I was about to find out.

As if he sensed my dark need, he put his fingers inside of me. "I've got you."

He pumped his fingers inside of me in a way I'd never felt before. The pressure built, and my body didn't feel like my own. Instead, it was his to command. My climax struck me like nothing else ever had. It was too much. My chest heaved, my muscles went tight. Then there was a rush of wetness.

A growl came from his throat. "Good girl."

"Did I—?" I'd seen it in porn but never thought it was possible for me.

He whispered in my ear. "You squirted, yes. And it was spectacular."

Fuck. He moved to clean me up with his tongue, tasting my climax. When his mouth moved lower, I froze.

"Has anyone had you here?" he asked, his magic fingertips fluttering at my pucker.

"No."

He swiped at the wetness coating my pussy and pressed a finger slowly inside. Every synapse in my body fired, and when his thumb pressed down on my clit, I was coming again. He swallowed down my scream with a kiss.

I was vaguely aware he'd inserted another finger, stretching my ass. "We'll play tonight. Need to work you in for my cock another time."

Another time. I clung to this statement far too strongly. It was impossible to pretend I wasn't ruined for all other men. Max was giving me more than my fantasy; he was giving me the care and trust in a partner I'd never had.

He moved down, kissing down my stomach, my legs,

before rustling with something. "This will be cold for a second, but it'll warm up. I want you to relax."

I gasped at the foreign sensation of something metallic sliding into my back hole. The thought of having Max there someday left me dizzy.

My ears strained to figure out what he was doing now. Soft footsteps fell, and I could sense him getting closer to the top of the bed. "Scoot up." He'd taken the pillow from under me and was now placing it between me and the headboard so I could sit up. "Open."

The one word caused me to hum with pleasure.

I wasn't the only one pleased. A hiss of breath issued from his mouth when he slid his cock between my waiting lips, and I started to suck. I sucked so hard he couldn't move for a moment. His hands tangled in my hair, and I could feel him removing pins from a long-forgotten updo.

His strokes were slow as if not to overwhelm me. Nevertheless, I was a vessel for him to fuck at his mercy. I slobbered down his length, my eyes watering at every inch he pushed further.

"That's it, gorgeous. Take it all."

Suddenly I didn't want the blindfold any longer. I'd rather watch him. I needed to see him come undone. I pulled off of him. "Remove the mask."

"Are you sure?"

I knew why he was asking. It was one thing to know you were being watched, but another to see the people spectating. It could cause me to panic. "Yes," I reassured him.

It took a minute for my eyes to adjust to the light. But once they did, I was thankful for the visual. His cock was perfection. His heated gaze locked on mine. I couldn't seem to look away. Instead, I was mesmerized by how he held me, both literally by the hair and figuratively by the power of his stare.

"Do you want to look through the window at the people watching? At the couple who are so turned on right now they're fucking against the glass?"

I wasn't sure how I'd react, but there was only one way to find out. I looked over. And what I saw had me mesmerized. Max was right. There was a woman in the window, her nude body splayed against the glass. An arm was wrapped around her and there was no doubt a man was pumping into her from behind. It was so unbelievably hot to know they were turned on by watching us.

"It's a private viewing room for couples. Figured we'd start slow."

I was grateful for him easing me into it. It felt almost intimate.

"Ready?" Max brought my attention fully back to him. His voice had a slight edge as though he couldn't restrain himself any longer.

"Yes." He was no longer gentle when he shoved his cock into my mouth this time. Instead he started pumping in and out with furious strokes. His cadence of deep, deep, shallow, shallow showed he was no novice at being deep-throated. He was teaching me the rhythm, and I was all too eager to be a star pupil.

"Fuck, baby, your mouth feels so good."

He was getting close. I could tell by the way his hips started to move erratically. What I hadn't counted on, however, was the vibrating wand he'd activated in his left hand and which he was now pressing against my clit.

Oh, God. The vibration was almost too much for my oversensitive pussy. But he didn't let up, and soon I was shaking as much as he was. When I climaxed, I clamped down, sucking hard, and a primal growl ripped from his lungs. Long spurts of hot salty liquid hit the back of my throat. Some dripped out of my mouth, but I didn't care. There was no room for modesty here.

I swallowed what I could before issuing the challenge. "Kiss me." He didn't disappoint, dropping the wand and taking my lips, not caring about the taste of himself on my tongue.

He kissed me down my throat, then up to my ear. "The audience normally likes something other than missionary for sex positions."

"I'm not performing for them. Only you." Yes, the couple outside the window turned me on; yes, I loved the idea I was being watched. But ultimately, I realized, without Max, none of this would live up to my fantasy. He was the element that made it so incredible.

He leaned back, searching my eyes. "You're sure?"

"Yes. I'm determined to make this bed a sex bed with you."

His chest rumbled, and he flashed a goofy grin. The type which had my heart tumbling. But I didn't have time to dwell on the kernel of fear taking hold. The one which told me that come tomorrow when this thing between us was over, I wouldn't be all right.

He freed the restraints, rubbing my wrists to return circulation into my hands before kissing each one with incredible care.

After the condom was on, he spread my knees apart. "This is only for us?"

I nodded, not taking my eyes off of him. "Only for us."

He pushed forward, entering me on one stroke. The sensation of the plug in my backside coupled with him filling me was incredible.

"One day I'll have your ass while I work a dildo into your pussy."

There he went again, making future plans. My mind knew it was pillow talk, yet against my better judgment, hope grew that this would not be our last time together. "I can't wait," I murmured, feeling him pull out before pushing back in.

He started moving faster now, pumping in and out, the sound of my wetness filling the room. My body, which I'd thought was down for the count after three orgasms, decided it needed more.

My legs started shaking. With the feeling returned to my hands, they grasped for his body. I needed more. I needed his lips. I pulled his neck down so he had to alter his rhythm, but I didn't care. I was starved for his kiss. For the intimacy. He seemed to need it too judging by the command.

"Eyes open and on me."

It was almost too much. The way he could stare into my soul and completely own my body. I shattered around him, attempting to cry out, only to swallow his moan when he took my lips. He slowed his pace, letting me down gently from my consuming orgasm.

"Did you?"

He shook his head. "Not yet. We're just getting started."

Holy shit. If I didn't survive tonight, it would be totally worth it.

Chapter Nineteen

MAX

After Oakley rode me on the chair, then I fucked her doggy-style, and next I played with her plug, I finally came hard and deep inside of her. I smiled when she collapsed on the bed. Orgasm number seven took her down for the count.

She'd been so damn responsive. Her ex-lovers didn't realize what a gift they'd been given in a woman so open to exploration while still so innocent. And the fact she wasn't performing but instead had been fully present with me—it was something I'd never experienced in any of these rooms.

Although she'd been turned on about the people watching, she'd still managed to make this experience about us. About what we both wanted instead of what was for the audience.

I knew without a doubt, tonight wouldn't be enough. She'd indicated she wanted a different future than my sister, which gave me hope. Hope that perhaps we could pursue something. What, I wasn't sure yet, but we'd be sure to discuss it.

But first I needed to take care of her. I fumbled for the remote to close the curtains to the private viewing room. I'd opted for a smaller audience since I didn't know how she'd react to things afterward. There was no one there now as I watched the curtains close. A glance at my phone proved why. It was almost four in the morning. The club was closed.

As much as I'd have loved to crawl into this bed and hold Oakley close, we were in a public room. She hadn't moved from her position and appeared to be sound asleep. So I disposed of the condom, removed her plug, and dressed enough for decency so I could carry her upstairs where there was a bedroom next to the office.

She stirred in my arms, wrapped in a sheet. "Where are you taking me?"

Her slurred words made me smile. "To a no-sex bed so you can sleep."

"Mm." She snuggled deeper into my chest.

Christ, I could get used to this. I'd never thought my lifestyle could sustain a relationship. I'd never thought I was missing something in my life until recently. But lately I'd been thinking about how empty my existence was. Sure, I had people who cared about me, but I didn't have my person. A partner like Shane had in Daniella and she had in him. Could Oakley be my person?

She hardly moved when I set her in the bed. Kissing her forehead, I murmured, "I'll be back." The room was private, and no one would disturb her up here.

Once I returned to the play room, I gathered up her clothes and other items.

Shane was waiting for me upstairs in the office, looking none too pleased.

"Who the hell is the girl?"

Considering he'd never known me to bring a stranger into the club, I wasn't surprised he'd ask. I just was hoping this conversation wouldn't happen until tomorrow. "Her name is Oakley."

He sighed. "That tells me so much. Why did you bring her to the club?"

"Why do you think?" I wasn't about to get into the details of Oakley's sex fantasy or how we'd met. I could explain as much as Shane desired to hear tomorrow after three cups of coffee and some rest. I was a co-owner of this club. Although bringing an outside woman in was out of character for me, I was well within my rights.

"Does tonight mean you're performing again?"

"Yeah, probably." Although it would be with Oakley and only if she wanted to do it again.

"Did she sign a nondisclosure form?"

We had an abundance of paperwork for members to sign before they could partake in the activities here. Legal protection. "She's someone I know, not a member."

His gaze narrowed. "Which is worse. Because if she's personally motivated to screw you over, then she can."

I shook my head. "I'm not dealing with this shit tonight. We'll talk tomorrow." He was in a temper, and I was exhausted. All I wanted to do was curl up with Oakley and get some sleep.

"This isn't like you, Max."

My fingers raked through my hair. "I know. Can you leave it?"

"Is this a one-night thing with her?"

"It was a weekend fling. I'll get her to sign the damn paperwork tomorrow." Although I'd already decided I didn't want things to end with Oakley, I wouldn't get into my plan to see her again until I spoke with her first.

He sighed. “Fine. How was the weekend otherwise?”

“As shitty as I predicted.” But at least Oakley had been there.

“Sorry to hear it. I’ll talk to you tomorrow.”

Chapter Twenty

OAKLEY

My eyes slammed shut the moment Max came in, while silent tears ran down my face. The open door had allowed me to hear everything.

I was only a weekend fling. He'd get me to sign some paperwork in the morning. He intended to start performing at the club again.

The words repeated over and over, not matching up with what I'd started to believe in my head. Incredible sex had made me a stupid girl. I'd known this had a deadline which expired tomorrow, yet I'd—what? Gotten my hopes up anyhow? I had no one to blame but myself that I'd been hurt.

Forcing myself to be still when Max wrapped his arm around me, I sighed when he pulled me close. If I'd been able to stand on my own two feet, I might've insisted on leaving, but I was hours away from convincing my body to go upright. So instead, I forced myself to relax, breathe in the scent of him one last time, and enjoy something I'd never have again.

It was still dark when I woke again, but I could see rays of sunshine start to peek in through the window. Max was turned toward me in a deep sleep. God, it hurt to look at him and know once he woke up, we'd have an awkward conversation. He'd probably go straight for the paperwork he wanted me to sign.

Nope, I wouldn't wait around for that to happen. I quietly moved out of the bed and searched for my clothing. I had to slip into the bridesmaid dress from yesterday as the only other option was the bedsheet. My bags were still in his SUV. So were my keys and wallet, unfortunately.

I located his car fob on the nightstand, deciding I'd grab my stuff, return the fob, and grab an Uber home. I hoped I could remember where we'd parked. Last night was a blur. A delicious blur which had me sore in many places.

Nope, I wouldn't go there. I eased the door open, breathing a sigh of relief when I saw no one yet occupying the large office. Slight problem, though. I didn't remember how I'd gotten up here, let alone know the way out. Crap. Well, there was an elevator on the far side of the room. I'd start there.

I went to press the button and wait. But when the doors opened, a beautiful redhead was standing inside, wearing jeans and a black heavy coat.

"Hello," she said, her eyes wide as she stepped off.

"Hi." I could imagine how terrible I looked after last night, on top of which I was obviously sneaking out in a walk of shame.

"You must be Max's friend."

"Yeah. Hi, I'm Oakley."

She gave me a warm smile. "I'm Daniella. My husband, Shane, is the other co-owner of the club."

I was relieved to hear she was married to his best friend. The thought of the other women he'd been with in the club was depressing. I was sure they were all beautiful like her, but at least she wasn't one of them. "It's nice to meet you."

"Where's Max?"

"Sleeping. Um, I was hoping to find his car, get my things, and go home." She looked like polished perfection, and I felt like a dump standing next to her.

"You sure he wants you sneaking out?"

Oh, boy. This stung. "One hundred percent."

"How about I show you where he parks, so you can hand me the key fob after you fetch your things and not have to come all the way back with it?"

"That's really nice of you." It also cut down the chance of Max waking up and the inevitable awkward scene to follow.

Daniella led me down the elevator and through a familiar corridor. "I assume, given the dress, you were in the wedding Max went to?"

"Yeah. I was." Thinking about the fallout with Kate started to make me sad.

"Did you two meet this weekend?"

"Actually, I've known Max since we were kids, but I guess you could say we got reacquainted."

She glanced over. "How was the weekend? Was there any drama with Max's family?"

"Yeah, unfortunately there was. It's why we came back early."

She sighed. "I hate that for him."

"Me too. He deserves better."

She gave me another look. "Where is home for you?"

"Jersey City."

"Oh, you're local, then."

"Yeah. I work in the Financial District. Do you work here at the club?"

She smiled. "Not officially, but I do the accounting because numbers make Shane grumpy, and I'm a CPA who enjoys them."

Interesting. I had other questions about what it was like to be with someone who owned a sex club, but we'd arrived at Max's SUV, and it wasn't any of my business. I opened the rear hatch and took out my suitcase, trying not to get depressed over the sight of his duffle bag. I also grabbed my purse and checked around to ensure I didn't leave anything behind.

"You sure you don't want to say goodbye to Max?" Daniella asked.

I gave her a sad smile. "No, we promised it was only for the weekend, and it's very clear that's all he wanted. Um, an NDA was mentioned, so if he needs me to sign something, maybe he could email it."

The sympathy in her eyes was obvious. "Of course. I'll let him know."

"Thanks, Daniella. It was nice to meet you."

"You too."

It occurred to me I could've asked to go back into the club so I could change clothes, but as I got into the backseat of the Uber still wearing my red bridesmaid dress, it felt like a fitting ending to the weekend.

Chapter Twenty-One

MAX

My arms reached for Oakley, wanting her warmth curled around me as a way to start the morning, but I found nothing but cool sheets. I sat up and looked around the room. Shit, she couldn't be gone. I had her stuff in my truck. But upon looking at the nightstand, I didn't see my car fob.

I dressed quickly in my trousers, not bothering with a shirt before opening the door. Shane was there at his desk drinking coffee.

"Where's Oakley?"

He looked up. "She went home. Dani took her to your car to get her stuff. Here's your key."

Crap. She'd left. As agreed, we'd spent the weekend together, and now it was over. I wondered if she regretted last night. If she was ashamed of what we'd done in the room for others to see. Or if she'd simply decided the weekend was all she wanted from me. Or perhaps all of the above.

"Did she say anything?"

He quirked a brow. "Like what?"

"I don't know." I dug the heels of my hands into my eye sockets, my brain not yet firing on all four cylinders.

My best friend and business partner stared at me in surprise. "You like this girl, don't you?"

"Yeah, I do."

"But earlier you said—"

"I know what I said. I just wasn't ready to talk about it. I still haven't figured out how it would work."

"How what would work?" came Daniella's voice as she stepped off the elevator.

I immediately peppered her with questions. "How was Oakley? I mean how did she seem? Did she say anything? Leave a phone number or something?" Jesus, what was I—in high school?

She shared a look with her husband before taking a seat beside him. "She seemed a little sad to be leaving, in my opinion. She said you had a rough time at the wedding, and it's one of the reasons you returned early?"

"Yeah. But given my father, no surprise. But back to Oakley, did she say anything else?" Something to give me hope?

Dani smiled. "You really like this girl, don't you?"

"Yes." And the fact they were both enjoying it while I was clearly miserable was annoying. Why had she left?

"I asked if she wanted to say goodbye to you, and she said no because you had promised it was only for the weekend, and that's all you'd wanted."

I let out a soft curse. Things had changed since we'd made our promises.

"Then she said an NDA was mentioned, and if you wanted her to sign one, you could email her or something."

I shook my head. "I never talked to her about an NDA. Unless she overheard Shane and me arguing about me not having one— Shit." I cursed, wincing at what else she must have overheard.

Shane got defensive under his wife's glare. "Wasn't as if I knew she meant something to him."

A moment of insecurity hit me. Oakley might not want what my sister did, but that didn't mean she wanted a boyfriend who worked every weekend in its entirety—at a sex club of all places. "It doesn't matter."

They both turned toward me. Daniella spoke first. "What do you mean?"

"I mean I'd make a terrible boyfriend."

Dani's eyes narrowed. "Bullshit. You're in your head again, Max. Don't make assumptions. If you want to see her again, then do so. If you want to try to make it work, then do it. At the very least, ask her what she wants before pretending you know what's best for her."

Shane spoke next. "Sounds familiar. Pretty sure you said something similar to me, telling me to pull my head out of my ass. I never thought I'd be the guy who took a night off or a honeymoon, but we made it work. And you can too. Don't you think this thing might be worth a chance? At least to talk to her."

"Don't you think if Oakley wanted a chance with me, she wouldn't have taken off?"

"I think if she heard you call her a weekend fling and you planning to start performing again, you might need to be the one who makes the first move." Shane obviously remembered as well as I did the damning things I'd said earlier in the morning.

Shit. "I meant performing again *with her*."

"Not what you said, though. And if she overheard you—?"

Then she would have assumed I meant with other women.

Shit, shit, shit. "I have her address." Thank goodness I had it in the GPS.

Daniella smiled. "Well, then, what are you waiting for?"

I returned her grin. Good question. I'd go home, take a shower, and practice what I wanted to say to win the girl.

Chapter Twenty-Two

OAKLEY

My Uber ride of heartbreak home was without incident. I went inside my little apartment, locked the door, and flopped on my bed. My four-hundred-and-fifty-square-foot studio wasn't much, but at least it was home. And everyone knew home was where you could cry your sorrows into a pint of ice cream. Or two. The nice part of living alone was I could wallow without interruption.

But unfortunately, I had no ice cream. Or food, for that matter—at least not the kind you wanted to drown your sorrows in. 'Cause let's face it, a frozen Lean Cuisine never made anyone feel better about anything. I closed the freezer door, dreading the idea of going to the store. But tomorrow was the start of the work week. If I didn't do the task today, I'd regret it all week.

First, I needed a shower. A long, hot shower where I tried not to think about Max's hands on my body. Afterwards, it was tempting to slink back into bed, but I needed empty carbs to fortify me through the night to come.

An hour later, armed with bags of chips, ice cream, two boxes of cereal and a gallon of milk, I returned home from the store. It wasn't long before I was sitting on my bed in my comfy clothes, staring at my phone and wishing for a text I knew would never come. Max didn't even have my phone number.

When Kate's number flashed, I hit ignore. I wasn't ready to speak with her.

She'd decided to judge me and then shame me. Nope, if I had learned one thing from Max, it was never to be ashamed again.

Thinking about Max made my chest ache. After last night, it seemed so strange to return to my mundane apartment and boring life. I'd been exposed to the neon sparkle in life, and now I was stuck with the matte, muted colors of mere existence. It wasn't just the sex. It was his humor, his boyish grin, and the way he made me feel like I was the most beautiful woman in the room.

So much for keeping my promises. I'd broken both by establishing feelings and wanting something beyond the weekend.

I exhaled and poured myself a monster bowl of Lucky Charms.

My phone rang again, this time from an unknown number. Hoping for Max, I picked up.

"It's me. Please don't hang up."

Crap, it was Kate.

"I know you're not ready to hear my apology, but I needed to tell you since we leave for the Bahamas today. Max told me about Shawn. About what he said and did to you, and I'm so sorry."

"I tried to tell you."

"I know. And I was selfish. And horrible to shut you down. I stupidly told Tim about the video when it all happened, and he foolishly told Shawn. We both feel horrible about it. I shouldn't have brought it up in front of Max. And I can't offer any excuses except to say I've been angry with you ever since you decided not to come home from college. I had this childish vision about us living next door to each other and always being best friends with our kids in our home town. I guess it's why I was pushing Shawn at you, thinking if you two got together, it would bind you guys to us as the couple we could always make plans with. I realize how selfish I was. I should've been supportive of you chasing your own dreams."

I stayed quiet, not sure what to say. She'd hurt me.

"Like I said, I don't blame you if you're not ready to accept my apology, or if you ever will be—" Her voice broke on the last word. "Just know I do love you. And I want what will make you happy. Okay?"

"Okay," I whispered. "I need to go now, but you have a wonderful honeymoon, and we'll talk when you get back, all right?" It was the best I could offer at the moment.

She was audibly in tears. "Thank you. I'll call you in two weeks. Oh, and if you and Max are together, then he'd be a lucky guy."

The mention of his name caused a lump in my throat. "Talk to you in a couple weeks." I hung up the phone and stared at it. Could I forgive her? Probably. Would the friendship be the same? No, but it wouldn't be even if none of it had ever happened. We wanted different things in our futures. We were different people.

Pouring the milk into my cereal, I took my giant bowl to my tiny couch and had just crammed my mouth with the first bite when a knock sounded on my door.

I got up and puttered to the door, gasping when I saw Max standing on the other side of the peephole. Unfortunately, sucking in a breath did not mix well with a mouth full of Lucky Charms, and I started coughing.

"Oakley, are you all right? Can I come in?" came Max's concerned voice.

Oh, God, leave it to me to be choking on Lucky Charms with wacky squirrels on my fleece PJ bottoms and a tank top with no bra when my dream man showed up at my door. Deciding I'd prefer to have the Heimlich than die, I opened the door.

He immediately thwacked me on my upper back, allowing me to breathe again.

Sexy I was not. I crossed over to my kitchen to retrieve a napkin and finish my coughing fit. Finally able to talk, I said, "Thanks. Guess you've come to the rescue again."

Dammit, he would have to go and flash those dimples. His gaze dipped down toward my braless chest.

The girls decided to show off by putting on their high beams. I crossed my arms over them. "What are you doing here?" Looking gorgeous in dark jeans and a gray sweater.

"I came to talk to you." He looked around my shoebox apartment. It wasn't much, but at least it was clean.

"About signing the NDA?"

"No, I never wanted one."

"I heard you, Max." It was impossible to keep the hurt out of my voice.

He stepped closer, lifting my chin so I had no choice but to meet his eyes. "What you heard was me giving convenient answers to my business partner at four in the morning when I was unprepared to answer his questions about you."

"Which means what?"

"You weren't a fling. And I was never going to ask you to sign an NDA. I trust you."

"You said you'd probably start performing again."

"Yeah, if it was with you. I wanted to talk to you about it first. I didn't know if you enjoyed it or how you're feeling about it." He sighed. "Shit, I'm bungling this. Here I had it all planned out."

Hearing he'd planned something made my heart beat faster. "Try it again."

He perked up. "Yeah?"

I'd meant for him to start over in his speech, but I had to laugh when he walked out my door and closed it. He knocked again.

This time I yelled out, "Just a moment!" I then whipped off my PJ bottoms, pulled on jeans and a plunging sweater. Lastly, I pulled out my ponytail scrunchie and fluffed my hair.

I opened the door. "Max. What a surprise!"

He grinned, taking in my outfit change with a raised brow. "Can I come in?"

"Of course." I ushered him into my apartment. "What are you doing here?"

He leaned in to whisper in my ear. "Not sure why you bothered to put on more clothes when they're about to come off shortly."

I smirked. "You're awfully sure of yourself."

He straightened up, the sidebar over. "I missed you this morning. I was hoping we could talk."

"Talk about what?"

"About more."

My lips parted. "More?"

"Yeah. I want to take you out on a proper date and spend more time with you. But I realize it would involve some sacrifice on your part. I'm the owner of a sex club, although maybe for the first time in my life I'm learning to be unapologetic about it. But it does mean I work weekends, late nights, and with women I've slept with before."

I swallowed hard. "Do you want to sleep with them again?"

"Nope. I want to be a one-woman guy from now on."

"Gosh, I hope that woman is me; otherwise, this entire thing is awkward."

He burst out laughing. "I hope it'll be you."

"I can't promise I won't get jealous from time to time, but I don't know...maybe Daniella has some tips."

"I'm sure she does." He rubbed his thumb over my bottom lip. Then he kissed me. "Oakley?"

"Mm." His lips behind my ear had me shivering with anticipation.

"Will you go out on a first date with me?"

"Absolutely. After you make good on your promise and get me out of these clothes."

Chapter Twenty-Three

MAX

Our first date consisted of picking up Philly cheesesteak sandwiches and heading to my loft apartment. I normally guarded my space and didn't invite women to my loft, but bringing Oakley there felt natural. Better than natural. It felt like the beginning of something special.

"Your place is beautiful."

I saw the exposed brick walls and rustic leather sofas through her eyes. I'd wanted Aspen ski lodge meets industrial chic. Basically, I liked being comfortable. "Thank you."

I set out dishes on the small dinette table and brought us two beers. "This all right?" As far as first dates went, it wasn't fancy. But the thought of taking her to a crowded restaurant wasn't appealing, either, because I wanted her all to myself.

We both ate in silence for the next few minutes, only commenting on how good the food was until I had to say what was on my mind. "We need to talk about some more things."

She took a big bite of her dinner. "Sounds serious."

I wanted to ensure we were on the same page long term. "I don't want kids."

She chuckled. "Then let's agree not to make any, okay?"

"I'm serious. I had a vasectomy years ago and have never wanted children." I didn't scorn those who did, but I didn't see a family in my future.

"Good. Because I don't want kids, either."

"You're sure? My sister sort of indicated you'd picked out names together."

She rolled her eyes. "Yeah, when I was twelve, and it was fun to play make believe and wonder what our lives would be like in the future. Contrary to popular belief, not all women want to be mothers. I've never had the urge, and I don't think it'll ever change. To be honest, I'm not sure about marriage, either."

Neither was I. Yet I'd seen it work for Shane and Daniella, so perhaps it wasn't off the table.

"Did you enjoy what we did last night at the club?"

Her blush was adorable. "I did. A lot. But you should know that unless it had been with you, it wouldn't have lived up to my fantasy. It was you who made it perfect. Left me thinking I might be ruined for all other men in the future."

Hearing I'd ruined her for other men gave me a possessive pleasure. "So much for our promises about no feelings and not extending past the weekend. I'm completely falling for you, Oakley. And although I can't promise I'll always be the best boyfriend considering my work schedule, I'm willing to give it my best shot and make you the priority when we do have time together."

She laid her hand along my face. "I'm falling for you too. I think together we might be able to figure this relationship thing out. How about we start by agreeing not to make any more promises?"

"Unless they're dirty." My waggled brows made her laugh out loud.

"Of course. Dirty promises are always welcome."

EPILOGUE

MAX

The weeks of Christmas and New Year's were the busiest times at the club. Shane and I typically took turns opening and closing, but during those two peak weeks, we operated on little to no sleep with every minute spent working.

I'd never minded the hours until this year. Until I had someone special waiting for me at the end of the night. Oakley had moved in with me last month, and as a result, was experiencing firsthand the reality of a live-in boyfriend who spent all his hours at the club. She'd been a good sport, but what I hadn't counted on was how much I fucking missed her. Especially tonight on Christmas Eve.

At least the club was closed tomorrow. I intended to spend the entire day with Oakley. She'd decorated our loft with a beautiful tree, and our stockings hung from the mantel. I loved the idea of spending our first Christmas together.

Over this last year, I'd also started talking to my mother

again. It had been baby steps at first, but she'd finally broken free of my father's decrees and asked for a new start with me. I was on board. Oakley helped facilitate the bridge we built, for which I was eternally grateful. I could have gone the rest of my life without speaking to my father, but I'd missed my mom.

I was excited to call her over the holidays and tell her the big news. Assuming Oakley said yes to the proposal I planned to give her tomorrow. She was already my partner in all things, but I wanted her to be my wife.

I counted the hours until I could go home, meanwhile working the bar and strolling the main floor to ensure everything ran smoothly.

"Room twelve needs you, Max. Something about the bed being broken," came Shane's voice over my earpiece. He was busy getting a dirty Santa and two of his naughty elves ready for the main event, so it was up to me to deal with room twelve.

"On my way." I walked off the main floor and buzzed into the hallway which led to the private rooms. I sincerely hoped the bed wasn't broken. Given the industrial strength of the steel frames, I wasn't sure it was possible. But if they had managed to break it, I'd have to see about re-accommodating the couple, a difficult task given how packed we were tonight.

After opening the door to room number twelve, I stepped inside to find a temptress in the high-back chair. Her dark hair fell past her shoulders.

"Thought you might need a little break."

My smile curved up at the sight of Oakley. Shutting the door after me, I hit the lock. "Yeah? So you arranged for a broken bed?"

"It's not broken yet, but we have exactly one hour to see

how much damage we can do." She stood up and peeled off the long silk robe she was wearing to reveal she was nude underneath.

I'd never get over how breathtakingly gorgeous she was. "I don't know how you arranged this, but it makes me ridiculously happy."

She grinned. "I had some insider help. Seemed only right to give you your first holiday gift here."

"Oh, yeah?"

"Now you just have to find it. Here's a hint, it's sparkling."

It didn't take long once I got her on the bed and began touching her to find the jeweled plug in her ass. Although this wasn't our first time doing anal, the fact she had prepped on her own and wanted to do it here was exciting.

"Best gift ever." I kissed her then, loving how responsive she was. I'd never tire of this.

After giving her one orgasm with my mouth, then another with my cock, it was time to take her ass. I did so face-to-face as I loved watching her expression. I applied the lube, wanting it to be comfortable for her.

The sight of her back hole opened up with assistance from the plug was so fucking hot. Sliding the tip of my dick in, I whispered, "Merry Christmas."

She moaned and retorted, "Nothing says holidays quite like anal."

I chuckled, which caused me to slip out. "Laughter and lube do not go together. Come on, game face on."

Now she was in a fit of giggles, and I was hard pressed to avoid joining her. Who knew sex could be both hot and hilarious? Yet I wouldn't change it. It was so unbelievably us.

I leaned down, kissing her deeply and saying the words I'd never tire of saying to her. "I love you."

Her lips tipped up in a smile. "I love you too. Now hurry up and put it in my butt."

I kissed her through my grin, lined myself up once again, and pushed in.

OAKLEY

I loved this man more than anything. Loved the way he pushed inside of me. Stretching, burning, yet feeling, oh so good. So forbidden. And because he knew how to amp me up, he whispered in my ear.

"Next time we do this, I'm getting us a viewing room so people can watch me fuck your ass."

"God, yes."

He slipped in further, taking shallow thrusts deeper while I adjusted to him. We'd played around with viewing rooms a few times over the last year, and it never failed to turn me on to be watched. But it was also important we have our alone time too. Like right now when I didn't want to share him with anyone else.

His shallow strokes started to go deeper until he was fully seated. My God, he felt incredible. I dug my fingers into his biceps as he ground into me. When his fingers went to work on my clit, I shattered into a million pieces. He followed, grunting and thrusting one last time to empty himself inside of me.

You'd think with all the orgasms Max had given me over the last year, I'd have developed more stamina, but nope, I was down for the count. As he pulled out, I winced with the aftershocks hitting my body.

"Stay there, love. I'll be right back."

I was pretty sure I couldn't have moved if I tried. My gaze focused on my handsome man walking toward me naked. The way he washed me gently made me fall even more in love with him.

"You okay?" he asked, kissing my lips as I got dressed.

"Mm, better than okay. Have a good rest of the night, and I'll see you at home?"

He smiled. "See you there, beautiful."

Max slid into bed in the wee hours of the morning. Per usual, I was naked and waiting for him. These were my favorite moments: when he came home, showered, and slid inside of me, making love to me slowly as though he'd been waiting all night to do so.

Hours later, I woke in his arms.

"Merry Christmas," he greeted.

"Merry Christmas," I returned, content in this rare lazy morning where we could both sleep in and spend the entire day together. Later we'd head over to Daniella and Shane's place for a Christmas dinner. I'd become close to Dani over the last year and considered her a dear friend.

"What time are Kate and Tim FaceTiming?"

"This afternoon about two o'clock. My mom will be with them then."

"Oh, good." I was so happy Max's mom was back in his life. It was like a weight had been lifted for both of them. As for his father, well, I didn't suspect that relationship could ever be repaired.

Kate and I had settled into a new form of friendship. It was a relief to have entered this next phase. The truth was we'd grown apart. But we'd found we could still be friendly without being involved in each other's daily lives. She'd settled into married life, and now pregnant life—due in mid-March—and I'd continued my life here in New York City, concentrating on my career in marketing. I'd even been helping Daniella lately on rebranding the club.

Kate seemed genuinely happy Max and I were together, and we planned on visiting the new baby this spring.

Max kissed my forehead. "You ready for your first gift? It's sparkly too."

"Oh, yeah?"

"Mm-hm. Do you mind reaching over and checking the time on your phone?"

Weird request considering his phone was closer. I reached out with my left hand to grab the device only to gasp. On my left ring finger was a beautiful diamond ring. My gaze swung to his.

He sat up. "Guess it was rather presumptuous to put it on your finger already, but I wanted to surprise you. I love you, Oakley. And I know you said you weren't sure how you felt about marriage, and hell, neither was I, but this past year has been the best of my life. I love our chicken nacho with guacamole and beer Monday nights, and our cheesesteak or shawarma Friday nights. I love coming home to you every night and knowing you're in my bed and in my life. I love the idea of forever with you as my wife. Will you marry me?"

I'd said I wasn't sure about marriage because I never could have imagined a partnership like the one I had with Max. I threw my arms around him. "Yes."

He took my lips in a searing kiss lasting until my stomach growled.

"I blame all that food talk in your proposal."

He chuckled. "Come on, let's get you fed."

I puttered into his kitchen, straight to the refrigerator, where I started taking out ingredients. "I have a surprise for you." I slipped a recipe card across the island toward him.

He quickly read it and looked up, his eyes wide. "Is this Dan's recipe for the famous bacon burrito?"

"It is indeed."

"If I didn't already love you, I'd be professing it for the first time right now. I can't believe you got Dan to give up a recipe."

"I have my ways." Those ways included promising we'd visit in April. My gaze focused on the beautiful ring on my hand. Max had outdone himself with the gorgeous rock. "They're going to flip when they hear the news."

He laughed. "Yes, they are."

Over our morning burritos, which weren't quite as good as Dan's, Max asked, "What kind of wedding do you want? Boxes with little bows which need to be tied the night before, or something different?"

He looked nervous which made it tempting to mess with him, but I wouldn't. "Honestly, I could go for just you and me on a beach somewhere. Maybe the immediate family if they want to come."

He grinned. "Thank God, because if you'd said you wanted a big wedding, I would've tied you up, kidnapped you, and smuggled you to a remote island somewhere to make you Mrs. Brooks."

Oh, snap. I suddenly had the makings of my next fantasy. "Promise?"

His gaze darkened, and he pulled me up out of my seat to lift me over his shoulder. "Christmas morning kidnapping fantasy coming right up."

Yes, please.

***

If you love the Dirty Duo, then be sure to sign up for my newsletter because I have an exciting MMF coming up in the future. Sign Up HERE

ABOUT THE AUTHOR

Aubrey Bondurant is a working mom who loves to write, read, and travel.

She describes her writing style as: "Adult Contemporary Erotic Romantic Comedy," which is just another way of saying she likes her characters funny, her bedroom scenes hot, and her romances with a happy ending.

When Aubrey isn't working her day job or spending time with her family, she's on her laptop typing away on her next story. She only wishes there were more hours of the day!

She's a former member of the US Marine Corps and passionate about veteran charities and giving back to the community. She loves a big drooly dog, a fantastic margarita, and football.

Sign up for Aubrey's newsletter to get all of the latest information on new releases here

Stalk her here:

Website

Facebook

Twitter

Email her at aubreybondurant@gmail.com

ACKNOWLEDGMENTS

When I first published Dirty Intentions I had every "intention" of writing Max's book in the near future. But near became further and further. Thank you for your patience for Dirty Promises!

I want to take a moment to thank some of the people who make my books possible.

Alyssa Kress! You've been with me since the beginning and made my books better one edit at a time! You're such a pleasure to work with!

Thank you to Kelly Green. Kelly is not only an amazing PA, but she's also my biggest cheerleader, especially when I need it.

To my ARC Team-THANK YOU for always making time for me!

To my friend Elizabeth Kelly: Thank you for the gorgeous cover! You brought Max and Oakley to life!

Thank you to Nikki Sloane for helping me brainstorm the "no sex bed" LOL

To Judy of Judy's Proofreading, what would I do without

you finding all of the little things? Let's never find out! Thank you for your eagle eyes!

To all of the amazing bloggers and bookstagrammers who shared Dirty Promises, thank you so much!

And last, but not least to my readers! Thank you for your enthusiasm for all my books. Love you all!

Made in the USA
Coppell, TX
04 June 2024

33125452R00085